M000078984

NOUNS
OF ASSEMBLAGE

HOUSEFIRE

HOUSEFIRE

2917 SE HAWTHORNE
PORTLAND OREGON
97214

www.housefirepublishing.com

ISBN: 978-1-937395-00-1

for
Gingey Mingey

CONTENTS

BIRDS

REPTILES AND AMPHIBIANS

A CULTURE OF BACTERIA

MAMMALS

A TOWER OF GIRAFFE

CREATURES OF THE SEA

AN ABOMINATION OF PLATYPUS

INSECTS AND SO FORTH

+

+BIRDS+
++

A BUILDING OF ROOK

by Matthew Simmons

God was followed everywhere by carrion birds of one type or another. No matter how he tried to fancy up, the smell—foreign, dead, weird—attracted the little gangs and groupings of them. The smell of him. The smell of God.

Trouble worked its way through that smell. It inspired some—and that's always trouble. It deadened others—and that's always trouble, too. But God couldn't eliminate it because it was just the smell of him and who can do anything—truly anything—about that?

So God and his birds walked around. They had taken up space in Turkey for a while, walked it Black Sea to Mediterranean Sea, day after day after day. And somewhere in Sinop, a man beat his wife to death! And somewhere in Sivas, a poem was written! And somewhere in Tarsus, the vermin evacuated a house, spilled out into the streets, and the birds descended and ate.

When bored, God set up a tent and waited for visitors. When visitors arrived, God pulled off whatever bird had taken to his shoulder and snapped its neck and cooked it. For the

3

visitors. God ate once an eon.

When edgy, God walked again. Turkey from end to end. And every pace God made was perfect. Exactly the same distance. People waited for him to move out of sight, and they scrambled to the footprints. They measured the footprints, and they used them as a standard unit of measure. The God Yard, they called it. Five God Yards in a Shining. Ten God Yards in a Perfection. Cube a God Yard, make a box, fill it with water, and you had a God's Body, the primary unit of weight.

The Turks, with precise buildings built on a base of God's measurements, ruled the world. Cowed in their own country, as God walked up and down and back and forth and scared them and yelled at them if they got too close, they were feared and envied the world over because they controlled the standard weights and measures of the world.

And God and his birds walked and walked.

A HUDDLE OF PENGUIN
+THE FIRST NON-DEATH-DREAM+

by J.A. Tyler

To fall asleep I sometimes hold one hand in the other
and pretend as if one of those hands is not mine but his,
or my mother's, someone who cared enough to hold me.
Somewhere down deep, longing is shaped like birds in trees.

In these woods, I wake to dreams.

I had a brother. I was a deer. These are the moments holding
me together.

In these woods it is death-dreams and daytime, the two
moaning in similar light. But then there was this first non-
death-dream, where the world was icebergs, where I was
crushed on all sides by penguins, where being a deer meant
nothing.

There was ice, and my hooves went slip-slip.

Waking from anywhere to here is bruising.

In the dream that was not a death-dream the cold was
frostbite on elbows and I couldn't feel any hands touching

my hands. I was only a person and not a deer-brother and the penguins were all the small feelings I'd ever had or wanted to have.

In these woods, where dreams turn forests to Antarctica.

I shiver and wake and we comb through these pieces.

A penguin is not a word or a feeling or a cloud. A penguin is an iceberg-cold moment. A huddle of penguins is a mass of sorrow. This kind of non-death-dream would be better served as a warm sun above a house built from trees, lit by a timber-heart.

A CAST OF FALCONS

by Megan Lent

The ragged, pointy edges of rusted shopping carts dig into our ankles as we race them down the aisles. We are eight-and-a-half. When we race, I sit in the basket and you push the wheels. We whistle under fluorescent grocery store lights. Sometimes we get free cookies from the in-store bakery, and other times we pop balloons, and other times we run back into the store-room, which is refrigerated, and practice biting our ankles with our teeth and scratching them with our fingernails to accustom ourselves to blood.

The crystal glass reflects the scotch on your wall and your computer, and I play with your hair and apply mascara to each of us. We are thirteen next month. I take a sip and admire your perfection. I accidentally say "confection," and you think I'm saying "erection," and the confusion continues until you suggest I make candy canes and hang them on your body parts—which you tell me are perfect. The idea appeals to me, but I do not let on.

The seal is granite beneath our secondhand boots, and we do not trip, no, we crouch forward into our new desks. We are fifteen. We do not race anymore; we are calm, we are cool.

We are prime. Our high school has a mascot. It is the falcon. You want very much to be the person who wears the falcon suit and runs around holding flags at basketball games, but you hear that it gets very sweaty in the suit, and when you tell me this I feel a clawing against my hips from the inside.

We are two weak fawns, our legs clamped together, in the dark under a tree. You are young. Queen Elizabeth The First had falconers: men who wore leather bracelets and sent falcons out to hunt things for sport. Eventually, the men would wise up and want to let the birds free. So they'd let them go. But, as it is with everything—from getting seduced by a phone psychic to witnessing childhood to taking a boat across the Atlantic in the body of a former friend to pretending not to watch you change into your pajamas as we sit quietly on your bed eating popcorn and singing to the radio—there is a catch. And the catch is this: they clip the falcons' wings. They can go, but they cannot fly. They are free, but they are also not.

The next time I see you it is a dream and we are both wearing thick sweaters, even though it is summer, and we are covered in a blanket of cigar smoke, and we are in someone's backyard watching a man and a woman.

She says, *like this?*, and she slips off her yellow shorts. They get stuck on some of the water spilled over from the deflated kiddie pool, and her feet—tawny, a dirty word, aqua nail polish, she smells like cold cream and hand sweat—pick up blades of grass as she curls her toes. He says, *yes so nice so nice just be slow, be calm, be normal.* He flicks on the red light and affixes the camera to the tripod.

Okay, he says, *now gyrate. Educate me,* he says, *like we're in a workout video. Help me step-in-shape. Ooh yeah. Oh, oh now we're getting somewhere.*

She peels the cotton off of her shoulders and rotates her neck back, allowing her muscles to contract, detract, extract. She wonders if she remembered to separate the whites from the colors in the laundry cycle at home. She wonders if she remembered to close the lid to the washing machine. She runs her fingers around her neck and ignores that they feel lightly scaly, and her hands grow tighter and tighter until her tongue is squeezed out like one of those penny-squishing machines.

You pinch my shoulder as we watch her sink to the ground and bow to the camera and piss herself, but I refuse to look at you.

A LAMENTATION OF SWAN

by Robert Duncan Gray

I.

Picture yourself as one of two strangers, thumbs upturned to the world outside, sitting at separate booths in a classic American diner which can and should only be described as static.

I am the other.

An aging waitress whose name tag reads Maggie, and is consequently a stranger to nobody, shuffles over to your booth. With one eyebrow raised, she waits for you to speak first.

"What's good?"

"Ma'am?"

"What's good here?"

"Folks seem to enjoy the caribou."

Your gaze travels over the menu.

"I'm gonna need another minute."

"Anything to drink in the meantime, hon?"

"A coke."

Maggie floats on back behind the counter and tends to her business, whatever that is. I seize this moment to make first contact. As I approach, the jukebox Loves Me Tender.

"The caribou's tough."

"Excuse me?"

"The caribou. It's not tender like you like it. It's tough."

"Maybe I like it tough."

"Nobody likes it tough."

"So what do you recommend?"

"Well, it's not on the menu, but I know for a fact that she just got some good swan in. Maggie knows her way around a swan better than anyone else in this city."

"Better than at The Grande?"

"Vladimir? He knows how to prepare a fine swan, ma'am, but the fact is that they get shitty swan. Pardon my French, but fuck The Grande. The swan here is usually no better, mind you, but I know for a fact that they just picked up a particularly fine lamentation on account of the fact that I just sold it to 'em."

I sit down opposite you and we are no longer strangers.

II.

We share each other's bodies now.

You know I prefer it when you don't shave. You know that when I see the thick hair that grows in your armpits I am reminded of your cunt, which is a part of you I like to be reminded of.

I know that you don't like to suck cock by the look on your face when you tell me you like to suck cock. I like having my cock sucked, so I don't say anything.

To me, you are impossible. I ejaculate at just the right time. The last time this happened I was young, still in school and more in love with myself than anything else.

Low on money, we share meals. Often we find ourselves back at Maggie's place. I compile a list of items we share:

Swan.
Snake babies.
Pygmy marmoset.
Electric eel.
Lion heart.
Battered tarantula.

Maggie likes us, even though we don't tip well. One time we

fuck in the bathroom during business hours. Afterward she tells us she listened at the door. She asks if she can watch next time, perhaps join in. I think it's a fine idea. Sure, she's a little over-the-hill, but whatever. Her armpit hair is light and appears to be soft. The contrast would be interesting. You're not game though. We tell her thanks but no thanks.

We are no longer welcome at Maggie's place.

III.

You are growing tired of me. I know all the signs.

I whittle a ring from an ivory tusk I find in a dumpster behind the bowling alley. I intend to take you out on a date somewhere classy, perhaps have the waiter hide the ring in a piece of cake or something. My plans are not set in stone.

I sit in a rocking chair and watch you sleep, thinking of the various paths our partnership could take from this moment on. Perhaps you will wake up in a moment or two, horny. I will know what you need by the look in your eye. We will make passionate love. I will cum inside you. We will share our diseases and, perhaps, bare a child.

This does not happen. You fart in your sleep and turn over.

IV.

I give the ivory ring to a homeless lady who sits on the corner of 5th and Main. She nods her thanks and says nothing.

I sit alone on a park bench watching the ducks, wondering how much I could get if I wrangled them up, snapped their necks and took them over to Maggie's place before remembering that I am no longer welcome at Maggie's place. For this, I blame you.

My plans are now set in stone.

V.

You will leave me within the week. I know this to be a fact as I lie next to you in bed, pretending to sleep, listening to you snore.

I move with the precision of a factory worker. Exit the bed. Dress in silence. Leave my letter on your bedside table and a bucket of water on the ground where I know you'll find it. I have nothing to pack.

My gaze travels over the room.

In my pocket I have the cigarette lighter I found on the floor of the public restroom in the mall. We were there last week to browse the selection of fossils at the fossil shop, but didn't end up buying anything. The lighter has a portrait of Elvis on it. Today would have been his birthday.

Your nightgown is made of faux silk. I have read the label. It is highly flammable, which is why I bought it for you. I suppose I have been planning this for weeks. I look from your nightgown to Elvis and back. I'm all shook up.

My plans are set in stone. I move like a machine. This ceremony is sacred to me.

VI.

Dear You,

My love is huge. Like, orchestra huge. There is nothing I cannot cremate and I am sorry for these things and the other things too. I will never forget the lamentations we shared. I have swallowed a dozen snake eggs, which I expect to hatch inside my stomach before sunrise. I suppose we will meet again soon enough, some place else.

Love, the Other Stranger, Me.

A PITYING OF TURTLEDOVE

by Caitlyn Laura Galway

It was a slanted fort, with pillowed walls of couch cushions, mattresses hung with tattered pink drapes like peeling skin. William huddled in a bathrobe he had taken from some suburban trash. It was covered in stains, possibly from toothpaste, but probably not. There was a long stare to him now, his hair greased in strands thick as string beans. And those cheeks, so sleazy pale, like pitted avocados.

We sat surrounded by the junkyard. William couldn't take his eyes from the snow. He thought the sky was flaking, told me to stop shaking my hair. He said "Be still. Maybe it's me," and scratched his scalp. "I've left dandruff over the whole city."

+

New York hit me like a steel cobweb when I first arrived. Clusters of skyscrapers, a blitz of car horns and bleating conversations. It was my first time in a city like that. There seemed such disconnection amidst so much movement; a place of electricity, without a single star in sight. And then I met the man with no shoes. William. He liked to feel the act of walking, said you knew each step when it was bare. He had his group call him Jupiter. They took me to a gathering in the basement of The Willowdale, a bar with a jazz band and a tinfoil wrapper buffet. All night he watched me and I pretended not to notice. He named me Turtledove and slid his palm along my back, calibrating the reluctance of my spine.

Soon I was painting him protest posters, all roiling with colour and heat. He kept close during rallies, bracing an arm in front of me whenever the crowds shook. His fingers crawled between mine, tied in a rope beside his, a barricade of us along the cinema's gate. The cigarette a cast of ash between my lips, my hair swept up inside a black beret. "You look like a fierce French poet," he told me.

+

I walked in on Francesca, one of Jupiter's girls, pacing in The Willowdale basement. Jupiter sat at a fold-up card table, scribbling her image into the surface. She was topless, pensive, one arm across her breasts. She seemed to take each step on a tightrope in her mind, one foot in front of the other, concentrated. She had her curls thrown up in a scarf with her fist to her mouth, eyes flat as Picasso's broken women.

I realized that I could never walk around bare in black nylons like that. Jupiter looked at her and looked at me, and I knew he wished I would. I felt small in my grandfather's steel-wool sweater, like I couldn't find my own way out of it. "Let's float in the river," Francesca said. "That'd get people's attention."

"Do you think they'll get it?" I asked.

"All they need is a reminder of death," Jupiter said. "They'll think of the war the rest of the day."

I checked my watch. "Where is everyone?"

"Late." He laughed a low, double-edged cackle.

Francesca kept pacing around the room. She muttered into her fist, tapping her cheek with her thumb. Her voice was buttered in sensuality even when muffled. "Fucking hippies," she said. The two of them began spooning meat sauce from a can and it left a red sore on her midriff. Jupiter ran a finger over it, then through his fluid hair that swam about his head.

He tipped the can toward me.

"Eat up, Karina."

He had such a way about him then.

+

"I want to take a bath with you." He leaned back against the mattress patchwork, his Frankenstein's monster fort.

"No, Will."

"I want to see what happens to you underwater." That wasn't as cryptic as it sounds. He just wanted to see my hair float. How my legs and arms sank, like marble sculpted around bone.

"You're frightening to look at next to snow. Where did all your colour go?"

"You're going to die of something awful, Will."

He pulled a pipe from the bathrobe pocket. There was a new cut on his lip, shaped like a starfish and flowing green and yellow below a glassy surface. I wanted to dip my finger in it. Maybe I could have hooked an organ, saved some part of William from himself. He tapped the pipe against his lawn chair. Disillusioned micro-bits flew out and chased the snow.

"Look at you. You're so fucking sad and sweet, you look like *childhood*."

"You and I are going different ways, Will." I kept my eyes to my boots as I turned to walk away. There was a dead bug caught in one of the laces.

"You look at me when you're talking to me, little girl."

But I couldn't. His eyes were like glaring undulations on a lake. He coughed and coughed with a sore, parched sound, and it was hard to watch him, be near him, right down to the smell.

"You and I are going different ways," he repeated. "That's a beautiful phrase, you know, Abigail—*You and I*. Two lonely words slipped together." He crossed his fingers over his knee. "See you soon, Turtledove."

See you soon.

I sighed. *Yeah. Probably.*

A MURDER OF CROW

by Tyler Gobble

The lawyer floats in the lake, in the center of town, formerly the city pool, formerly the water treatment center, formerly a hole in the ground. The concrete edges crumbled, sunk. The fence carried off, replaced by waist-high grass.

He floats and thinks. He stares at the sky and thinks. His wife will leave soon he knows. She had her hand on his partner at the trial this morning. Someone had been murdered. A triangle they were—he, his wife, the partner—their side shorter.

A waterbug flicks near his ear. The sound like his daughter's inhaler as she wheezes in the back of the courtroom. His shouts weren't about the judge's idiocy or the witnesses' bullshit; it was about his wife and her hand and the leg of his partner. He saw them in the lobby afterward. He saw them in his office last week. He saw them in his living room a month ago.

He mimics the bug and flicks his wrists. At first, the water felt cold. At first, this situation froze, the courtroom, the table under his sweaty palms. He shivered for the first time in years. His daughter high-fived his partner, hugged his wife, nodded at him. Out the doors of the courthouse, he followed a few feet behind his daughter as she walked to school. As she stepped inside, he waited for her to peer through the little window in the door. She didn't turn around. He turned, left.

He listens to the beating hearts of the things swimming and crawling below him. It exists—the water and its creatures and the tufts of his suit unraveling. Sinking is a thought he has. Wind blows between the houses and shakes the surface. He floats towards the center. He closes his eyes to see what the lake sees. The fish in their families, their schools, his body unraveling into the deep green.

Above him, some caws. He opens his eyes and crows fly in the shape of his wife's face, smiling.

A COMMITTEE OF VULTURES

by Jarrid Deaton

The Judge runs his index finger along the ridge of the vote-meat that I brought him, the sun-bleached spine clicking under his fingernail.

"Caddy, this here, as you know, is a groundhog," he says. "If you want to be my bailiff, you have to slink up the food chain better than this."

The Judge is up for reelection, and I want to be his new bailiff. We are up against Elder Grindrod though, and Scatter, his bailiff-in-waiting, has already turned in vote-meat from deer, turkeys, and a sloughed-skinned horse.

"The Committee wants something new this session, Caddy," he says. "What I need you to do, what it's going to take for me to slide my robe over my shoulders again and for you to be my bailiff, is to bring me the kind of vote-meat that will go down in history."

I made the mistake of starting a family. Most bailiffs-in-waiting avoid plug and pumps for their own betterment, but I married Notty and then gave her the pregnant belly six months ago. That means I have to become a bailiff to bring man-support to the table.

I back up against the wall of the Judge's office and grip the side of the door. I do a corner whirl and I am out in the hallway and heading down the stairs to start the search for better vote-meat.

I drive to my usual spot on the highway and look for dark spots in the distance, fur being wind brushed, and I finally eye a deer, its ribs still moving, sucking in that brushing wind. By the time I get my tools prepared, Scatter slides by on his state-issued four-wheeler and crushes the deer's skull with his fat tires. He slings a rope around its neck and drives away, a whole mess of lost life littering the highway. That's how things work. I can only blame myself for being slow with the tools, for letting my looks linger too long on last breaths and waving fur.

I am thinking both clearly and muddled when I get home. I watch Notty shuffle toward the fish tank in the living room and drop some flakes in the green water. I think about our child inside her, but the more I look, the more her growing belly seems bloated with the magic of roadkill, a miracle rotting under the sun. I think about something else as I get my tools prepared. I think about the most important thing.

A MURMURATION OF STARLINGS

by Ashley-Elizabeth Best

I've always been scared of rooms engulfed in the false, blue
fog that televisions deliver best. When mother turns the
television on, a pulse builds in my ears so that I think it
must be some speaking heart, a last little lust thrown out on
a magnetic wave. I sit in front of the T.V. table with my T.V.
dinner every night with mother. Digestion is the only work
I refuse to do, and so just before eleven I reheat my tray and
give it to her. She's been inside so long her face has gone
the colour bones go in a stream. She's so large and brittle,
trawling the same route through the house.

Sometimes I want to tell her to empty her brainpan, to once
just tell me how she feels. Instead I yell, *Momma I was trying
to describe you to someone yesterday and the only thing I
could say was, 'Her knee aches when it is going to rain.'* She
just cups my chin in her dank spongy hand, eyes smirking
like she has an answer I've forgotten.

When the night's yawning peal sounds (eleven O'clock news),
she rocks herself up to her unsteady feet and goes to bed. I'm
left a never-sleeping heap on the couch. When I know she is
fettered to her dreaming self, I pull out the ring from my left

shoe, kiss its opal rise, and begin my furtive walk about the house and out to the tree.

This is my ritual. How could I dream it, this descent, weathering the star-eaten sky, the river about my neck. I wash momma from my throat, even though I know she will keep me, and I'll keep her, no matter where I go or what she does. I am her memory of light firebolting ever away.

There's easy virtue in this: calling to a cadaverous love who will never come. I collapse beneath the tree, after it's all said. In the sky I see the slow-fading blips of stars—most likely satellites. I can hear the starlings' feet scraping the branches delicately, abandoning the frost that consigns the tree to a slow sleep. To live stelled to your roots is to voluntarily live in hell, to contract that long echo of memory, the false remembrances that enable me to recognize the truth. I kiss my ring just before dawn, giving the dead some time before I scare off the birds, again.

A PARLIAMENT OF OWLS

by Matty Byloos

This is the way that judgment always happened.

A committee was formed and rankings were established. The owls wore black robes and each one clutched a prop. One had a monocle and a speech impediment. Another smoked a pipe, fondling cancer right there in his beak. Still another carried an aluminum briefcase attached to the base of his claw with a bracelet like a handcuff. His entire existence had been a secret to the rest of them.

A harlequin of dancing owls. One owl stumbled over the idea that quite a few books were worthless, finding no solace or comfort in language on the page. This was when they had still been looking for answers. Two owls discussed what had been happening in the new New America, in the wake of The Motorcycle Gang's arrival. Nobody on the committee was eager about anything before. They realized there hadn't been any freedom in the beginning, and that the end would be different. They hurled themselves into the end like a blanket over an angry fire.

Three owls were careful to admit that society was conspiring against them. The Motorcycle Gang's presence had changed everything. They were suddenly as meaningless as the currency circulating through everyone's hands. Four owls wrote simultaneously on four sides of a damp pad of paper. *The sign of something interesting is in fact that it can absorb many forms of criticism.* These same pairs of owls wondered where the voice had come from, wondered who or what had inspired the words. It was The Motorcycle Gang, breathing into their consciousness.

Five owls maintained silence in a gesture of solidarity that lasted almost fourteen minutes. Realizing the futility of their actions, they each gave in to speech once more. They gave in to uselessness. They said they were sorry.

A pity of owls, an apology of owls, more sincere than ever before.

A braid of six owls chanted the words to a speech their predecessors had penned the last time the country came together in unison to agree on a collective purpose. A sophistication of owls. A fluency of seven owls spoke in a tone that evinced no doubt: together, they intoned, brown cannot win. the triumph of brown comes from being the last to die, and brown cannot win. Eight owls agreed that every society receives the criminal that it deserves.

A rotisserie of debating owls. A limitless chaos of owls. A wholesale departure, an evacuation of nine owls resigned their posts, for they considered what was happening to the country to be an event of savage purification. They staged an exit. Ancient scrolls were rolled up and briefcases were closed and locked. They wrote no letters, convinced there was so little time left. A fleeing of owls took to the sky, and the light of the afternoon diminished.

A shadow of owls blanketed everything on the ground in a mess of dappled charcoal gray. A screaming of owls. A cacophony of anxious owls. A foreign kind of humming sound, like a life from inside a vacuum cleaner or turbine, rose up over the entire city. The people gathered in the center of the square around the giant tree, felt the cool of a restless tornado overhead; some lost their balance. Collective equilibrium became disrupted for the moment. A contract of owls. And then, it was calm once more. The parliament of owls abandoned their lives of watchfulness over the people and escaped into the tired sun, never to be seen again.

A STORYTELLING OF RAVEN
+OR AN UNKINDNESS OF RAVEN+

by Colleen Elizabeth Rowley

"They flood our minds, seeping into our moments of purity
for the Lord, and branch by branch they build their nests!"
His chest rose and filled with vindication.

"AANNND . . ." he said, making sure to stare at each teary
eyed lost soul.

"WE ALL KNOW what happens when they build their nests.
They fly in, one by one and PECK AWAY at the divine until
all that is left is the cold darkness!"

The women shook with fear, the fear of knowing that they
might have a branch that has been slowly building into a
nest, that they too might slip and let on to their children
about these twigs and branches. But their men held them
tight, knowing that if they let go that their arms may turn
into wings, and those nests inside their wives would be all
too tempting.

So they stared, stared at the mother who had let her child see
too much of the night.

"What they have left of the body of this boy shows nothing
but picked over life!

Of dark shadows born upon the uncertainty of God!
THIS IS WHAT IS TO BE FEARED
This is a storytelling of raven!
An example of what God is not!"

It was the gentle kindness that he no longer had, staring him in the face. He could not take away from this animal what was slowly escaping from himself. He knew his choice. The wheel jerked sharp to the right, the gravel slid under his tires, he could feel his heart beating heavy, until there was no more ground to run from.

The weight of his body was gone. Gravity had lost its purpose and for a moment everything was frozen. He took in one last deep breath, exhaling as his body was broken against the trees he once thought were his friends. They were no longer friends, but watchposts to look upon the fast moving reality. His bones shattered into thousands of tiny little pieces, leaving his body limp.

They watched the fire break the night sky, eating one layer of reality after the next until time and space melted onto one another, forming a shade of black that only they were familiar with. His flesh and blood boiled inside his capsule of skin, forming a thick tar that hugged close to his tiny little bones. The air took in one deep breath, swallowing what used to make up this boy, breathing out a thick black smoke of fervor. Pools of blood began to pour out of his crusted skin. Ash fell from the smoke, thickening the blood into connecting shapes.

They knew this mold; they had all come from it.

"When you see the darkness, do not look into its temptation

to understand it or to know it!

NO, it is to be feared, to birth only impure thoughts!

YOU must look into the sun! Stare at it until your eyes flood with light, until God is with you even when you close your eyes, until you see no darkness! And when all you see is light you must burn those creatures of night!

You do not know them
They are not God's love
They are not your children
They are not your hopes

They are everything that is wrong with this world, everything you do not know!"

He rose from his ashes, from the darkness he had always been warned of. Wings spread further than the light he could see, touching what was soft and welcoming.

"Beware your thought of darkness; do not give light to the creatures of night! They are our enemies, demons set upon us to tempt against the almighty will and way of eternal happiness and righteous power of God!"

Eyes looked upon him from all angles, with no doubt or needs, feeding him with what the humans were afraid of.

This was no unkindness of raven, this was his family.

+

+REPTILES+
+AND+
+AMPHIBIANS+
++

+

A FLOAT OF CROCODILE

by David Doc Luben

Claire leans against the hood of her car in the parking lot of a highway attraction boasting The World's Largest Alligator. Claire suspects there are a number of important distinctions that make one creature an alligator and another a crocodile, something to do with skin composition and amphibianism, but in her mind she has made this simple. The difference between them is the same as the difference between a beautiful woman and an ugly woman: an alligator is longer and thinner, and a crocodile is fat.

The World's Largest Alligator is a crocodile. It is very fat and tall, with puffy paws and dull, threatless finger bones. Also, it is made of plaster. It is a cheap plaster building, the size of one or two railway cars.

For a few minutes, between seeing the billboard and getting there, she imagined a living, snarling thing, a gleaming leathery phallus with teeth and knowing, circular eyes, writhing in the shallow swamp waters inside its flimsy cage. She imagined reaching her hand toward it and being warned by the uniformed hunter not to get too close, but she would get too close, and the alligator, which would be an alligator and not a stupid fat crocodile, would be fast and bite her hand clean off. Her hand would snap like a doll's, leaving a clean, smooth stump. As she drove she bent back her hand and rubbed her wrist, trying to feel how it would be once the hand was gone. She would tell her next lover about it, how her hand was eaten by an alligator, without mentioning the alligator was in a cage. She could hide all other stories inside of this one. Talking about the alligator could take the place of talking about her previous lovers, though the story would sound just the same, and she would tell it with the same omission. She would imply that she had been surprised and attacked and barely escaped, not that she had just walked up and fed herself to him.

Instead, The World's Largest Alligator is just this big, plaster building shaped to look like a crocodile, faded green paint and crooked plywood letters lying about its species. She walks right into its faded mouth, but it does not bite down, and inside is a gift shop. The air smells like stale water and freshly kicked gravel.

Behind the counter a girl in black stockings waves at her, in a tired and polite way that makes it clear she is not inside of an alligator. Claire looks at postcards, but they are the same postcards as they have at all the gas stations. She asks if there are any real alligators. The girl points toward a shelf with a peeling plastic aquarium.

Claire presses her nose against the plastic. There is a baby alligator inside, the size of two fingers. It has dark skin with one bright yellow stripe across the face, and it is sleeping inside of its water dish. She can't even think of a part of her small enough for this alligator to bite off. A nipple?

The shop girl comes over and lifts the hatchling out, puts it in Claire's hand. She had forgotten that "cold blooded" is not just a metaphor. The alligator's skin is cold and stiff, and Claire remembers being allowed to visit her Granny in the funeral home, and how she touched her Granny's face and it was cold and stiff, and she wanted to ask why would a dead person be cold, why wouldn't they just be the temperature of the room, but it seemed like something that would be rude to ask, not respectful, so she just touched the skin, and could see up close that her Granny's mouth had been glued shut. They glue your mouth shut, she thought. They close your eyes and glue your mouth shut, so that you can lay there dead and look peaceful instead of terrified.

Claire holds the alligator in her palm and wonders how something alive can be so cold. She wonders how something so small can feel so strong. She thinks for a minute about slipping the alligator into her pocket and running to her car and raising it in the kitchen sink and the bathtub until it is big enough to eat her hand. But what would she do with it then? Once you let someone eat even just one part of you, they will always expect more. We all know what happened to Captain Hook.

But that was a crocodile.

The shop girl shows Claire how to hold it by the skull, with her thumb keeping its mouth closed. The alligator's mouth has been held closed so often by so many people, it does not even fight anymore. But the shop girl says, do not let go. It can move so much faster than you think. If you let it latch on to your skin, it will not be easy to get it off.

A HAREM OF AXLOTL

by Lindsay Allison Ruoff

1.

He'd taken up residence at the Imperial Motel because he was The King. The road to his kingdom was desert in the company of its conquests: the remains of sea creatures, shells, coral, oysters—the skulls of triumph over a different vastness. He'd once been a salesman of watertoys and floats.

His throne was a reclined beach chair, poolside. His skin resembled the membranes of oranges before the groves were gone. He and the sun, the trustiest member of his court, waited seasons, burned through memories of the shadows they'd made together. The King rarely touched the water. He didn't need to, owned it.

Summer people would eventually tumble through like thirsty dust bowl Okies. He watched for the youthful women, the girls, to slip from their towels and submerge their skin. Sunblocked and oiled bodies, fish with gangly arms, they slipped about and wrestled with his waters. He fought them, dove into their pores, made them exchange liquids, made them liquid, until their temperatures adapted and each stroke looked like a dance just for him. From his throne he'd chew a crusted lip with satisfaction. His pets in his aquarium.

They could never see his eyes, the eyes which drank them up. He hadn't seen his eyes in years.

2.

The rock in the sky shone down on them and made their insides shift, tides.

"We are sitting in a place that has been completely cut in half."

"So many times."

They looked from the mountain, which at one point had been just a pile of rotted rags, over a town with lights and buildings and manmade water. The northern half seemed to mirror the southern.

And leaning together one said, "But everything just grows back."

3.

She assures you that she comes from a long line of performers. Her mother conducted the fleas and her aunt danced with ropes and air over pits of hungry alligators.

"I've got no problem breathing under water," she said.

The lake is cold. You can tell just by looking at it. Sunlight only catches the top couple feet. She doesn't wear shoes, even on land, and eases herself onto her back, pushing off from the shore. Her dress keeps her afloat for a moment as she draws open her accordion fold by fold.

"Return to me," she sings with the first exhale.

She sinks slowly. The sound, that old sound, creates a current in the water. It rings and squeezes between soggy reeds. You imagine it is hard for them, the reeds, a struggle to pulse and bellow while being drowned. But with her they do. Her arms grow stronger, move heavy water in strokes. The opal sheen of the instrument matches her skin, scales. Sun plays along their surface, makes the eyes gold and she is almost out of sight.

It's so slow and soft and you almost don't notice how small she's gotten. The bubbles stopped but you think you can see her tiny lips moving and the song fades or travels slightly in new waves. You hear it still though, her external lungs pumping.

You wait and listen until you can't listen anymore. You know she has gone backward somehow, from land to water. You want her more than ever now—to be with you. But you can't disturb her.

A RUMBA OF RATTLESNAKE
+A LOVE LETTER TO A TREE+

by Janey Smith

On one side there was Edward. On the other there was a room. Edward was neither inside nor outside the side on which the room was. Obviously. Nor was he inside or outside the side he was on. And this made him a curious figure. For Edward never took sides, keeping politics to himself. Still, he was neither opposite the room nor alongside it. Nor next to it. It might be more accurate to say that Edward was not outside the room at all. But nor was he on the side the room wasn't—the room's side being somewhat indeterminate. Which doesn't mean that Edward was without room. Or for that matter that he was the room itself. He wasn't. Edward could, however, go wherever he wanted—and he oftentimes did.

Even on the night he left his room—the night, which was odd, could not contain him. It could not provide the frame around which a figure of Edward could be determined. Thus, permitting an outline of Edward to come into being for a moment on a truly gruesome night. The night was there, no doubt, but not really. The night had its own place, which was not the place Edward was. And yet, it was there.

The room that Edward left that night—that night during which there was no night—was not the room on the other side of Edward. Edward didn't have any sides. He wasn't flat, he just didn't have them, never took them, but had, of course, plenty of room to do so. His leaving—and what followed—was something else, though.

Let us leave Edward—not as a prop or a place or anything like that but as something else, a real person—to the side to which he does not belong. Let us just let him be there. Let us pretend. Now, even there Edward is not there. Not on any side. Not at any place. Not a prop or a place, but a real person, Edward, for now, is Edward. But that is deceiving. Edward would be the first to tell you that he is without doubt not equal to himself, and that, here, he is not alone.

The room was there, though, that's for sure. Not there specifically, generally speaking, but somewhere else. Always somewhere else. And this didn't bother Edward, because he was there, too. Not in the room, but there, where the room was. Which isn't to say that when he was there he was inside the room. But that at one point, perhaps, there was a room and there was Edward. And they faced us. They faced us without breaking anything. Without even looking at us. And this made them strange. But only for a moment.

The moment passed the moment it was named, of course. But, its name seemed to come before it. So, it is hard to say that it was even there. Most likely, it wasn't. Moments like this—and perhaps like all moments—never seem to last, really, but they also rarely ever come into being. That is—just what they are. In other words, even before the moment became what it was, it was something else altogether. In other words, neither this nor that nor both this and that, but something mysterious and difficult to name. Moments tend not to move us at all, which doesn't mean that each and every moment is an impasse, or that we have a right to our disappearance or to the disappearance of others. It's just that such moments have such lasting effects. It's hard to tell.

So, Edward left. Which doesn't mean that he left some place. He didn't. He didn't leave any place. Nor did he go anywhere. He left no place and he didn't go anywhere. Edward left, though. And it wasn't as simple as it seemed.

Furthermore, no place could contain him. Not even that place outside the place that could not contain him. There was Edward. He was there. There, here, being no place, but not the kind of no place we are used to. A very different kind of no place. Really, a place without one. A place without a no place, but also without a place. Which isn't to say it was placeless. There was something there. It was just difficult to place.

One more thing, this may sound like we're repeating ourselves, but Edward—despite what has seemed to be described—didn't take a side. There was no side. Neither one side nor the other. No sides. So, no here and no there. No opposite sides. And no non-opposite sides, or just plain sides. None. But, Edward had to start somewhere. So, he put himself there. Provisionally. Provided that there were no sides, which there weren't. Merely an Edward and a room. Just kind of there.

Repeat: Merely an Edward and a room. (But, just kind of there.)

A closer read may show that the "and" here—that is, there,

up above, but, now, also before us—does not do Edward or the room justice. If we can speak of justice. For lack of a better word. Because the "and" puts Edward first before the room: "Merely an Edward and a room." This is what this "and" does. By no fault of its own. One can't help "and" in this way. Its omission does not solve the problem.

Merely an Edward, a room. Or Edward, room. Edward room.

And neither one of them, the phrases above, gets us closer to the simultaneity, proximity, closeness, the relation of Edward and room. Their taking place at the same time, same place—but without time and place, whichever came first—and without taking anything, really, makes their special case a peculiar problem. To which neither of them got very close. But, close enough it seems.

I don't know.

It might be tempting to say that Edward is flat. That the room is flat, too. We've already dealt with this possibility. This would make them definitive. Fashionable. Almost acceptable. Maybe even popular among certain segments of the reading population. But, let us be clear that neither Edward nor the room are measurable, or flat. That both are, in fact, beyond measure. And for good measure, really.

There was Edward, there was room. Same time. Same place. But, not really. It was impossible not to put one before the other, to not place one before the other. So, let us pretend. Here, let us pretend that what is pretended is real.

Let us put the room aside for now—but as if there were no sides. No sides at all.

There was Edward and, being somewhat unhappy with himself, there was Edward. Two Edwards. Both at the same time, same place. Where are they? They are there. No place, really. Really. No place. But not the kind of no place we are used to. Neither seen nor unforeseen. But right before our eyes. Two Edwards. Both on. The real deal. Both matter.

And there was a room somewhere else. This will be our setting. This room that is always not there. Always somewhere else. Without place or position. Nowhere we are used to. Without where or care. Not there. Not even there where there might be one. Just a room. Now, picture a room without room. Get the point? A room without room that is also pointless. And two Edwards. Near, but not next to. Not beside. Near—now listen closely—if and only if it were not something we could say is near, but something else. Something strange.

Both Edwards were, indeed, strange. Not monstrous. Just strange. And like the room also pointless. But, not how you think. There was Edward. There was room. Here and there. But not far off. Edward is here. The room is there. They were close. Indubitably close. Closer than we'd care to think. Closer than, say, the two Edwards were. The two Edwards being merely hypothetical, to make a point. That is, almost pointless. But never a disappointment. And like Edward, dissatisfied with his job, always late. Which isn't to say that Edward was behind the room. Or that he lagged behind it. The room was there. Always. And this constancy coupled with Edward's nagging persistence allowed Edward to be there, too. But not how you think.

Let us come back to the room that is not there. Like Edward, our setting. The room, it should be said, was not some abstract thing. It was real. Right there. Although just how close it was to Edward is a question difficult to answer. But, it was there. And, like most rooms, the room that was there was heavy-bodied. It had other characteristics, too. But understand this: the room in no way, shape, or form resembled a person. Or a body. Not least Edward's. It was heavy, though. But, not situated. Not frozen in time. It didn't possess the kind of gravity you read about in fashion magazines. It possessed a gravity all its own. Something closer to a snake. If Edward got too close, the room would vibrate, warn him to stay away. And Edward—as we have seen—got close. Really close. Before Edward left he oftentimes did things to bring the room even closer. Like, right now. He is moving fast, putting his hips into the room without so much as entering it. The room backs off. Edward pursues it. All this without so much as moving a muscle. The room, which is there and not there at the same time, but real, is there. But it is impossible to know if Edward knows this. What we can say for certain is that the room has the capacity for it. But, Edward is another thing. But not the kind of thing you are thinking. He doesn't have the capacity for that.

The room. You probably imagine fours walls, a space, a door, maybe. Or a stage. Three walls and an open space. But, our room was nothing like either of those. It didn't hover in space. It belonged more to the night that wasn't there. And yet, it still moved us. Brought us to an unimaginable place. A place without place. Something fast, erotic, uninhibited. And although it was there without a door or so much as a window, it closed the door on Edward when Edward, almost without knowing it, left.

If it is possible to tell a back story about the room, it would be this: the room that was there was not there at all. And to attempt to place it, to somehow tell its story in space, which is, after all, impossible, would be to go backwards. And that, of course, is precisely what we are doing—without going anywhere at all.

This "at all" which gives us no room—and the closest description of the room possible so far—is a not very curious expression. It attempts to put "all" everywhere. To make its location total. But, this "all" can't be everywhere. Even in the special case of the two Edwards and the room, which are there—that much we know—and not there at the same time, same place. I mean, it's not like they are everywhere at once. That would be confusing.

Edward got close. How close we don't know. Perhaps too close. But he was there. And so was the room so far as we can tell. And neither appeared to the other as what they were, but as something else. Something else indeed. Before Edward left, the room closed its door without so much as having one. There was night. But not the kind you are thinking.

Let us be clear: we are not speaking metaphorically here. We are not speaking metaphorically at all. Not even close. Not even obliquely. We are saying that there may have been a moment when there was an Edward and a room. Edward was there. The room was there. But not where you think they were—if you were thinking anything at all. Because it's possible that that, that is, everything we have said and so much that has yet to be spoken, is not even possible. Which doesn't bring it any closer to the impossible. Only closer to us. Who are here, right now, but also far away, maybe—some place we may never know, or come together to find out, perhaps, despite being near—or nearer than we think.

Like Edward, maybe. Or the room. Close. But not in the way you are thinking. Not that way at all.

A MESS OF IGUANA

by Nicky Tiso

Your legs like bent garden hose chaffed by arboreal light
move in squat bursts, and when you move it is as if you are
repeatedly exiting a pool, for you seem a fish on its way
to becoming an upright creature, caught in the half-shade
of meat and frailty. Perhaps it is for your camouflage that
evolution has left you an ancient thing, with yellow, gray,
and lavender hues reticulating a hide clung to bone as leaf to
branch: with a quivering fidelity.

Your back, topped with a column of spikes ornamenting
your spine in varying levels of erection and recumbence,
jostle as you move among the canopy: the preponderant
marks of your aggression. Alluvium, your flesh the color of
what tropical sediments, dense foliage, rind of fruit washed
against it. Interlaced leaves polish your back, flood you
with a green too deep to analyze. You fall into lakes from
high above, rippling its surface with crater and scales—is
it placid enough not to clot your blood? So warm is your
environment, a gigantic festering circuit of pollen carried to
its end, in whose tides your tail propels you.

A BANK OF MONITORS

by Ryan Boyd

Summer journal, Day One. Today was hot. You know what you're going to get when it's like that. Hot days do it to all of us. Cracking tempers, cold showers, two changes of clothes when what you want is no clothes. That's how *Romeo and Juliet* starts. My grandmother used to call them "blue blazes," as in "hot as." *Hot*, from deep in the old German, like *ax* and *lick* and *cold* and *fuck*. It was hot, the sun a pasty hall monitor, watching everything we did under the palms— mostly sit.

When Saturday is that hot, you put out the bat signal and a picnic happens somewhere. My patio this time, on my mortgaged strip of lotus-land. Vinho verdhe, olives, brie. Well-planned. The coolers started sweating after a few minutes; two hours later the surviving beers bobbed in slush. God it was hot, so hot we felt watched. We water-watched: across the street a neighbor's sprinkler threw out spruce, banded water. Summer makes you think about sex more. Kiss me. I'm crude as the weather and love you in skirts and didn't want to stop, but like I said, friends were with us and they probably didn't want to see it.

Here is a way I tried to start a poem once: *summer is an apparition of lemon, lager, gauze, an indolent pause between blossom and burn.* It was a bad poem. Still, I have studied and transcribed many summers.

When I was a kid we cured this kind of heat by swimming back in the hollers where creeks come down and get together. Diving into certain deep waters that fall off the mountain like cold blood from stone gashes. The Moon Spring pool, a favorite, took my feet and legs and all of me with a cobalt grip, fear-glossed and intimate and swift. When I hit the water the dead were watching, it was that blue, and when I came up I brought their salutation to my boys on the bank.

California isn't supposed to get muggy weather, dammit. *Muggy.* Now that narcotic slur of a word is a little poem about this heat, this weather you damp the page with. Weather drinking pink wine out of cups. Sky come down a pestle, the air is leaking drugs. Rump weather, soft-boiled weather, loose angles and fat doors. Hay fumes off the lawn. There's charcoal and the stoop. Weather feral with itself and dying of its fruit. In another life I might have monitored the weather for a local TV station until getting fired for drinking on set and saying shit like this.

Like most backyard gatherings, ours got boring after a few hours, despite the good people. I began to feel obscurely responsible for this—I often worry that my friends are one crudity of mine away from realizing what an asshole I am and erasing my phone number—but your friend's boyfriend bailed me out by standing up, with the elaborate care of someone four drinks deep, and demanding that we *take this to a bar.* Everyone was down. I declined, got teased a little, then wished everyone a good time. Should have wished them luck, because at a bar you know what you'll get. I like bars but they're the worst.

Say you arrive early, just as happy hour is starting and only a few shadows sit around peering into their phones; maybe just as a game is starting on one of the flatscreens above the bank of bottles and the Coors Light mirror. Ready to tip back the contents of the late afternoon's gold cup, plush and slutty as the first ripple from an incoming buzz, you put your elbows up on the bar's greasy wood as your belly blooms. If you're lucky, a girl is pulling pints; if you are very lucky, she is one of many free agents in the place. There are ways to go about it with manful aplomb. Trust me, a sensitive pervert knows. So approach calmly, because you are complicated and subtle and can impress her with the breadth of your reading. Be a man of good plans.

Actual recon is bad: they'll be sipping vodkatinis with boyfriends, or nervous, dumpy coworkers who make you sad and bored at a glance, and anyway by the fourth pint and the third cigarette you probably have a nail drilling behind your eyes and just want to go home and smoke a bowl. By halftime it's clear your team has lost badly, and worse, played a boring style. Your buzz crumples into a cooked posture, your brain flickering. Bars are the worst.

So I didn't go, and stayed in my backyard as the sun cruised over and then into a bank of privet. I have good talks with myself here. Born nerd, I admit it, knowing nothing public beyond the standard charms anyone can fake, I look for honest responses from the green stuff in my yard, answers that are considered and loving. Wordsworth was right: one of these days nature is going to tell us exactly what kind of people we are. I have worked this swatch of land, sinking bulbs, chopping the soil, wetting it, shredding my back to lay out the patio's brick quilt, nudging and thinning the canyon oaks, laboring to make it my place among the seasons. This leads a person to worry about the weather and to feel himself a hair in the green scruff that beards the earth, even in the suburbs, which is where we are.

A LUMP OF TOAD

by Robyn Bateman

The fat white one rolled over. The couch shifted under his weight, and he picked the basketball shorts from between his ass cheeks with quick precision. "A lump," he said decisively. "A group of toads. It's a lump." He lifted his leg and ripped horrible ass, clouding the room with what reminded Marvin of old egg salad and cooked beet water.

"If a lump is two or more toads," Marvin exhaled as he scratched the skin between his left testicle and his thigh, "then I could say the sky was lumpy on the day it rained frogs in Egypt. *The third plague blackened the heavens with lump*. Why didn't they say that?"

"Because it didn't rain frogs, idiot. Is that how you've pictured it?" His chin glistened with pepperoni grease under the hot florescent lamp Marvin's mother bought for the dormitory. "Prob'ly just flooded the Nile. Overflowed with frogs or something. Gross."

Marvin sat for a moment in silence, plucking at the rubber buttons on a television remote. "I read toads have weaker legs than frogs, so they don't swim."

"Prob'ly," said the fat white one. Marvin kept his eyes half shut, trying to disregard the stack of urgent textbook readings on his desk. He pictured a toad in the middle of a white desert, its tongue as dry as its back, croaking at a mirage of its own lonely death. He shuddered and lit a cigarette. *At least there are two*, he thought.

+A+
+CULTURE+
+OF+
+BACTERIA+
++

+

A CULTURE OF BACTERIA

by Ryan W. Bradley

Tracy always liked to show me the pictures she took. She was a freelance photographer. When we first got together it was pictures of her, naked self-portraits, close-ups of her body parts. Now it was photographs of microscopic slides, pictures she was taking for some lab in town.

I'd been fired from my gig painting houses, so I was home while Tracy was working, which didn't happen very often. I slept for an hour and a half after she left. When I got up I took a shower. My morning erection wouldn't go down. I soaped it up, let the hot water beat against it until it was red as a cooked lobster. The shower was so hot and all my blood was in my dick. It made me see stars, like I was going to pass out. It reminded me of the petri dish images Tracy showed me every night. I got out of the shower and brushed my teeth. I walked around the bedroom, my dick still hard. There was a pair of Tracy's panties on the floor in the closet, next to the hamper. I picked them up, held them to my face and inhaled, saw her spread-legged before me. Saliva built up in my mouth. I held the panties tight in my hand and went for the dresser. I sifted through her underwear. I rubbed them on my erection. Soon, I had pulled out all the panties.

They littered the bed and the floor. A pair was hanging from my dick. All that was left in the drawer was a purple dildo.

The last time I'd even thought of Tracy's dildo was when we were first dating and she emailed me a picture of her using it. I hadn't ever thought of asking her to get rid of it. I hadn't thought there could be any need for it. Didn't we screw day and night? I stared at the purple monstrosity. I stared at it like it was another man hitting on her in a bar. I slammed the drawer shut and laid on the bed. I smelled the panties from the floor. I wrapped clean pairs around my hard-on and began to jerk off.

It was like an anger fuck, but less satisfying because I kept seeing the purple pussy eater. I kept seeing Tracy going to town on herself like the apocalypse was coming. My dick went soft.

I stood up and opened the drawer, grabbed the dildo. I held it and tried not to think about the differences between it and my dick. The length. The heft. I threw it in the bathroom trash. Then I took it out and walked it to the big trash can out in the garage.

I went back to the bedroom and put the clean panties back in the drawer. I started to throw the dirty pair in the hamper. I held them to my face again, felt the blood surging. My phone beeped with a text message. It was Tracy sending me a picture. Before I opened the message I pretended it was like the old days. That it was a picture of her tits, rather than some slide of bacteria or her clowning around with some nerd in a lab coat. I closed my eyes, tried to get back to that image of going down on Tracy. I inhaled and tried to bring the world with me.

A CULTURE OF BACTERIA

by Robert Vaughan

As a rule, people avoided him. Whether he was bowling, in line at the ATM, or drunk-dialing his iPhone waiting for the M103 on Houston Street and Avenue A, they steered clear. Bar patrons even ignored him during a drag show at Barracuda.

Over time, he'd developed a laissez faire attitude. His mantra was "let it be," and he'd chant the chorus repeatedly like a koan. He grew a tortoise-like shell, masking his pain. Home alone, he'd don a wig, sculpt layers of make-up, using centerfold cut-outs from European fashion magazines for inspiration. He'd croon along with his favorite ballads, performing to cheering fans.

One summer night in 2007 while preparing his routine, CNN leaked the news: a senator was caught in a public bathroom. An idea came to him: what if I try his tactics with a twist?

He decided to give it a whirl in the toilets at Grand Central Station. He stopped by Wigs and Plus on 14th Street where the owner, Sunny, would sell him a cheap hairpiece "for his mother." Then he propped himself in the furthest stall from the door every Sunday morning. Wig in place. Like a parishioner. Or a TV evangelist. Or a congressman.

On the way home, he'd stop at Magnolia's for a cupcake.

"It's all about service," he'd say to no-one in particular while he devoured his dessert.

A CULTURE OF BACTERIA

by Len Kuntz

They grew.

They hung off me like coffee-colored leeches, like long stemmed loogies, like drizzled yolk or goo caught in the corner flap of one's mouth when it is pasty/waxy/dry but still fluid.

And they were menacing.

Evil actually.

Some looked familiar. One had a set of eight-ball eyes. Another had the fangs of the first Doberman who bit me when I was five and still a pussy. Others resembled my parents—Mom with her cat-eyed glasses and Dad with his razor-sharp flat top, hands tucked in his lap so as not to show his dirty fingernails, his filthy self, to finger the lacey hem— upraised under his overalls—of the pink panties he wore at dinner.

At school I ate my own hair for lunch. I grew it long so I'd be sure to always have snack time. I sat in the back of the library and wrote, I AM INFECTED I AM INFECTED I AM INFECTED over and over, pausing with an occasional exasperated flourish, just in case someone was watching.

Now, I am married. My wife's a lot like you. She's normal and clean. She's plain-to-pretty on a sliding scale. She says, "We should get you checked out." Being vague is what women do, I understand, but still, her eyes waver when she says things anymore. Her skin has started to itch as well. She claims I'm contagious.

There's a movie called *Do The Right Thing*. I think about it a lot because I want to do that, I want to do the right thing. Hosts are supposed to take control. Parasites and bacteria can become more than a nuisance if left to roam free. Colds are catching. Most things get shared eventually—idle gossip, mouth spit, needles and faked laughter, STDs and mono.

So I've decided to be bold and go big. Nothing simple or sleek. I've got a hatchet. It's the chipped-handle one that my father once leveled next to my Adam's apple, the one with the faded red paint on the steel.

I have the perfect place for the blade. So many places actually.

I shall give this old axe a new coat of red. I shall end the spread of disease, this absurd madness. I will do what my ancestors should have done years and years ago.

A CULTURE OF BACTERIA

by Morris Hawthorne

New this fall to RealiTV, Channel 29!

HEY! YOU'RE NOT MY GRANDSON!
At risk youth get pulled from their bad neighborhoods and troubled home-life situations and placed into... Nursing homes? Watch as known thieves, gang-bangers, and sexually aggressive teenagers mix in with abandoned senior citizens all riddled with parkinsons and dementia. Hilarity ensues.
+ Thursdays at 9pm, 8 Central, right after SWAMP FUNERALS.

CREAMPIE CASTLE
One wealthy bachelor with an affinity for not pulling out hosts twenty female contestants in his four story, fifty room mansion to see who can take the most baby-batter without getting pregnant. Hilarity ensues.
+ Sundays at 7:30pm, 6:30 Central, right after THE BRIDE'S WAY OR THE HIGHWAY.

HAIR METAL AND THE HENDERSONS
The Henderson family opens their home to the members of 80's metal band ARSENIC, one member at a time, to

try and help them clean up their life, find Christ, and get their band back together. But what the Hendersons don't anticipate is how charming—or infectious—the band's satan-worshipping, heroin-slamming, and groupie-banging ways can be. Also, hilarity ensues.
+ Saturdays at midnight, 11pm Central, right before NOBODY'S DAUGHTER NOW!

HEY! YOU'RE NOT MY GRANDMA!
Inspired by Little Red Riding Hood, this show takes wolves and other large carnivores, dresses them in nightgowns, and places them in rooms with cute 13-year-old girls. You can bet that hilarity ensues.
+ Mondays at 8pm, 7 Central, right after WOMEN'S PRISON WARDEN.

FUCKED WITH A KNIFE
Real life rape/murder victims... who got away! Watch as they tell their stories directly to a camera with dramatizations of their awful experiences intercut with red fades and freeze-frames on tear-stained faces. Hilarity ensues.
+ Tuesdays at 9pm, 8 Central, sandwiched between two episodes of CHILDREN'S AUTOPSIES.

EAST COAST PAWN TATS CAKE STAR BABE BOSS
Follow the lives of the chef/tattoo artists who customize all their chairs and tattoo guns with hydraulics and flames and pinstripes, their sexy manager Veronica Sweets, the tough but fair boss who is currently working on a country album (on top of writing two books a year) and insists that all of her employees accept personal family items instead of cash in exchange for services, and her father Mustache Mike, the man who first revolutionized cake/tattoo/pawn shops in the late 1970's (more or less). Hilarity (and personal growth)

ensues (and how).
+ Wednesdays, Thursdays, Mondays, Saturdays, Fridays, Tuesdays, and Sundays at 6, 10, 11, 3, and 2pm, 5, 9, 10, 2, and 1pm Central, right before DR. NO LICENSE: BACK ALLEY MD.

Watch it!

A CULTURE OF BACTERIA

by Nate Quiroga

He entered her body. Like a three-day old shit. The hole dry
and the matter hard. It pushed through. Thinking carefully
not to disturb it, he closed his eyes and pretended it didn't
hurt. But it chafed at the corners, pulling the skin back like
hair from a scalp.

He pictured his cocktail waitress from earlier. Her white
skin curved down like a moon into darkness. He jabbed and
wrenched at her insides, jerking the organ, an ape-shaped
mechanic gutting the last car of the day. She wheezed in
ecstasy.

He remembered how he used to put it to her. Picking her
up, throwing her here, spreading her there, her limbs bent
in every symbol ever designed, from swastikas to stars of
David. Now they ate too much before bedtime. Their bellies
held two stones, grinding methodically, like two jaded boy
scouts waiting for a flame to catch.

He pictured the waitress again. The freckle on her
collarbone. The nose mousy beneath the eyes. His mind
skinned her and dressed his lover in her image. The body

jostled above him. It was the night before the fourth of July. The fireworks exploded into colors. He couldn't see them. Instead he pictured bombs falling, gun shots firing. A siren circled behind him and fell off toward the water.

He imagined holding a knife between his legs, cutting deep. He thrust into the mistress in his lover. It must have felt right to her because she squirmed like she used to. Her voice rose, clawed the air as if to strip the boards off the apartment walls. The idea multiplied inside him like a bacterium. Her ribs accordioned to surface, lips curved sharp into the shape of a sickle. The missiles fell closer and closer to their window. His chest jerked halfway up. The black dot at the center of the nucleus split and mitosis occurred. He wanted to throw her over, but she didn't get off that way. She sat on her heels and slapped herself against a man far away from her, hammering at his body, trying to bring him back.

He grew soft and she rolled over. The distant explosions faded. She wiped a towel between her legs and turned. Their backs touched.

From above they looked like two giant exposed lungs, each breathing at different intervals. Morning came. She went to work and he stayed in bed. Everything was fine.

A CULTURE OF BACTERIA

by Kirsten Alene Pierce

Fermier Johanson spread the toes of the student. "Here," he indicated somberly, "One may see a culture of bacteria."

Fermier was simultaneously excited and disgusted by his ability to annually select from among his forty to ninety pupils a student with a visible bacteria culture living on their person.

The student peered closely at the folds of speckled flesh in the crevice of his own greater and lesser digits. "Yes," he said, "Yes I see it."

"It's revolting!" said a member of the audience.

Fermier released the foul foot and sanitized his fingers.

For lunch he had spicy thai and a banana. Indigestion interrupted his four o'clock lecture and he dismissed the class (to great fanfare) twenty-five minutes early.

His wife called the office at half-past-six and told him she was having dinner with Paco. Paco lived down the street.

Fermier paid Paco thirty dollars to cut the front grass every week. This task took Paco less than ten minutes. Technically, Paco made more money for his time than Fermier ever would. Fermier did not find this emasculating. Fermier's wife talked about Paco incessantly. On the phone she told Fermier that she was going to a movie with Paco after dinner and that he should not expect her home until three at the earliest.

"That's a long movie," Fermier said.

"It's foreign," his wife replied.

At seven o'clock, the humanities secretary knocked on his door and jangled her keys in his face.

"Locking up," she said.

Her fetid, diseased breath wafted across the office, constricting the airflow and causing his lungs to balloon out in panic. The secretary had advanced gingivitis. Fermier gagged. The secretary's husband, Rich, had left her the previous September for a bulimic social worker. Rich and the social worker had traveled to India together from whence they sent postcard photographs of themselves holding skeletal children and building small houses.

The secretary bought a turtle and named it Rich. Fermier imagined that, when she was alone, the secretary would turn Rich (the turtle) on his back and prod his soft underbelly with the sharpened point of a pencil while his legs wind-milled slowly and hopelessly. Technically, Fermier thought, it was better to revenge oneself on a turtle than a man. On the screensaver of the secretary's computer was a close-up photograph of Rich (the turtle) and the secretary, nose to nose. Fermier washed his face and hands vigorously in the faculty restroom before leaving for the night.

Fermier, not wanting to be seen by any students, avoided the main campus walk, but behind the theatre building, the student whose toes Fermier had displayed to the class earlier in the day, approached him.

"Hey Professor Johanson," the student said, grinding the twisted butt of a cigarette into the thigh of the bronze Native American he had been leaning against, "That was cool, what you showed us in class with the thing in my toes, you know?"

Fermier nodded, trying to look as busy and important as possible.

The student was addicted to painkillers. He had been in and out of rehabilitation centers periodically throughout the last four years. That is where he picked up the habit of chain-smoking. If Fermier had known that the student had traded one for the other he would have had the urge to tell the boy that painkillers were technically less harmful to his body than unfiltered, hand-rolled cigarettes.

The student held out his hand. Fermier shook it. Walking away, Fermier tried to wipe his palm clean on the back of his khaki-colored business slacks.

Minuscule bacterial spores had lighted on his pink, clammy phalanges. They reproduced.

Fermier drove home in relative silence. At a stoplight he hummed "Jesse's Girl" by Rick Springfield.

When he arrived at his house the lawn was freshly mowed. His wife's car was not in the driveway, it was down the street in Paco's driveway. Loud music was coming from the house. All of the bottom floor windows of the house were glowing gold and yellow. Anger trickled down into Fermier's spored hand. The bacterial spores began to reproduce faster. Fermier did not turn on the lights in his dark, empty house.

Fermier turned on the faucet and was about to squirt a dollop of SoftSoap brand hand soap from the little penguin-patterned plastic dispenser when he stopped. He shut off the faucet and sat down on the couch, gazing at the fingers of his hand. Another flash of anger seeped down Fermier's arm and into his hand. The bacteria divided and dispersed.

Fermier prepared a mixture of sugar water and gelatin in a large soup pot on the stove.

When the mixture was warm, he turned off the burner and carried the pot into his bedroom. Fermier bundled the duvet into a large circle on the bed and poured the solution into the center. The gel set quickly. Finally, Fermier pressed the palm of his hand against the gelatin. It left a shallow, textured imprint.

Fermier scrubbed and sanitized his hands, the pot, the stove, and the steering wheel of his car.

At four in the morning, Fermier's wife stumbled into the room, naked to the waist and smelling distinctly of vomit. She collapsed onto the gelatin and fell instantly asleep. Fermier got some blankets and a pillow out of the linen closet and made himself a comfortable bed on the living room couch.

When Fermier awoke, he peered into the bedroom to check on his wife. She was engulfed in a sheet of thick, mossy fur; her bare breasts had sprouted a miniature forest, bisected by a plunging, mucuosy ravine. Her hair was a misty cloud of ash, and her torso bifurcated at the buttocks into two broccoli-plumes of spongy, constantly proliferating bacteria.

+MAMMALS+

++

+

A SLEUTH OF BEARS

by David Tomaloff

I could feel the forest breathing; I felt the gentle rise and fall of its belly as I awoke. Something was missing. There were no telephone poles, or satellites reflecting static back into my ears and eyes, but that wasn't it. The gaze of the sun felt light upon my neck—the warmth juxtaposed against the cool of the green beneath me. If the forest knew my name, she was alone in the knowing, and her secret was safe from my prying and half-hearted line of questioning. I listened to the ticking and the disquieted chatter of spectators who appeared to understand that I had at last rejoined the living. It was as if they knew why I was there—as if they were taking bets on what might happen next. Dressed down to the suit of clothes all beasts are born with, I began to wonder if civilization was but a dream. Had I dreamt the hustle of men and the noxious combustion of cars? Had I dreamt the cages man had fashioned for himself, or the security in knowing I was safe from the jaws of wolves as night descended from the heavens? And what of me? If my life was but a dream, it was one whose imprint was erased by the fragile light of morning and the scent of dampened leaves. My stomach growled as I righted myself to gaze at the sky placed just beyond the reach of the trees above. I will need a tribe, I thought, a gang like those I remembered from my dreams; a gang which would forage and howl, and sing songs of the myths of men. I'll have need for such a gang, I thought—by what name, then, shall we be called?

A TRIP OF GOATS

by Jamie Iredell

As a child my lunchbox was cast from tin and depicted
a Confederate Flag-bedazzled Dodge leaping over the
following: a police car, a Southern Belle, a fat man. Evenings
I sat cross-legged before a television spouting Dixie and
Waylon Jennings. My Hot Wheels rattled across the kitchen's
linoleum, smashing into one another, though none dented.

In middle school my sister's bedroom walls were held up by
posters of the New Kids. I got an earring. My father laughed
at it and said, "You look like a girl." I bought a pair of British
Knights and kept them white with cheap leather repair. Their
tongues flopped over the cuffs of my black Levi's. I got into
exactly three fights and earned a single bloodied lip.

In high school Randy turned me on to weed and Nirvana
and flannel and Mountain Mike's Pizza (all you can eat, good
Wednesday nights, after the parking lot bowl got smoked).
Then, just as quickly, Randy turned to Too $hort and The
Ghetto Boys and damn it felt good to be a gangsta.

I followed suits into college, paying my way with a Men's
Wearhouse job. My Givenchy, Louis Roth, Pierre Cardin, and

Hugo Boss came 40% off.

I found a bar. I quit my job to work at the bar. I've been drinking ever since.

I don't have cable television. I hardly drive. A billboard passes by the train's or the bus's windows and my head's in a book. I haven't a clue who sings anything these days. I wear New Balance tennis shoes. Sometimes I still hum Waylon Jennings, cause I'm a good timin' man. Got no woman with any kind of a heart.

A COLONY OF BATS

by J. Bradley

"Batman jumped the shark when he started franchising his vigilantism," said Michael, before covering his face with a spray-painted silver hockey mask.

"What do you think we're doing now?"

A GANG OF ELK

by yt sumner

My dreams hurt. They scratch the insides of my eyelids
and make my mouth so dry that I drink two giant glasses
of water a night in my sleep. I still wake up thirsty. I use
whiskey and vodka and wine with Xanax and pretty soon
no one knows what my drink is. You think it's cider and get
a hurt look when I order beer. I wake up naked with half-
formed memories of the sex we had. The dreams are much
stronger. Stronger than the joint we smoked before we fell
asleep because I knew even after the whiskey and sex the
dreams still might come. And they do. I curl up on my side
away from your warmth and watch the images flicker by,
some fading, some imprinting so hard my head begins to
throb at the left temple. I know it's going to be bad when it
throbs there so I rub the spot and squeeze my eyes shut. I see
blood. Taste the dirt. I smell cold sweat. I feel the hard bone
of my forehead break through and wind its way around my
head. It grows quickly and sprouts hard points that dig into
my neck. You shift and reach out for my breast, your fingers
working more adeptly in your sleep than when you're awake.
I clasp my hands between my legs and work in tempo with
the beat in my antlered cage. I think words I can only say to
other men. I think of your girlfriend in her bed and wonder

if she does this too. If she needs more and hides it from you. My breathing is shallow and the bones dig tighter in the silence of the early morning. I turn my head into my pillow and when I lift it the pillow is wet with my tears and the insides of my thighs drip with my orgasm. You wake up not long after and tell me you have to go. You kiss me and ask if I had any bad dreams and I turn back into my damp pillow and tell you no.

A GRAVEYARD OF ELEPHANTS

by Willie Fitzgerald

Despite the blood, despite the deer with enormous fangs; despite their wholly unconventional wilderness guide; and despite what would be decided, later, in a civil court as massive punitive damages for emotional and mental distress of a certain party; despite all of those things they arrived atop the mountain, and for at least a moment I bet they felt pretty good, pretty accomplished.

Here is what happened:

They left from Base Camp, which had a parking lot. The parking lot sold bumper stickers. They said: This Car Climbed Mt. Impossible, or This Person Climbed Mt. Impossible. This second one was actually an iron-on patch, not a bumper sticker. Sorry. At Base Camp you could rent a wilderness guide for the afternoon. That was me. Base Camp also sold iodine tablets and postcards of deer with enormous fangs. The deer were made-up, like the Jackalope from the mountain states, except the deer were entirely terrifying.

Halfway up Mt. Impossible and they stopped to have a drink of water. You could pretty much do Mt. Impossible in a day, up and back, but that was if you didn't really want to enjoy the scenery. The pioneers who had named the mountain hadn't really had any perspective on mountains. It snowed on this mountain sometimes. That was pretty impressive to them.

As they sat down—they had been hiking for three hours now—they decided to eat some granola bars. In most situations this is a pretty safe maneuver. Eating granola bars, that's a pretty solid action to take. Except that a deer with enormous fangs was like BANG, it was like right there. It got one of them, the lady. It got her pretty good. The deer buried its head in this lady's stomach. Blood was just shooting out from around the sides of the deer's head. The man, he was staring and holding his granola bar saying "Oh, Oh, Oh." I didn't know what to do, but I was wearing a uniform. I had a knife on me, so I sort of approached the deer. Just then the deer turned to me! It had a chunk of long stringy guts in its mouth. The woman was on the ground and white and with blood gurgling out of her mouth. She was not looking good, no. The deer shrieked at me. I didn't know they made that sound. Mostly we shoo them out of the parking lot or fence them off. Those deer, the parking lot and fence deer, don't have fangs, so far as I know. This deer had pretty enormous ones. The postcards lowballed them, I think.

I made myself large by grabbing the lower front corners of my wilderness guide waterproof jacket and raising them above my head. I bet I looked pretty big. Unfortunately it was pretty awkward and then the deer shrieked again and I stepped backwards and tripped over something. I was on my back, and the deer walked towards me. The man threw a rock at the deer. The lady was still saying pretty much one letter, over and over. The deer was on top of me, and I got hit in the head with the rock. I was alright, but still. The deer turned to the man and the man locked eyes with the deer and the man just said, "Please." The deer reared up on its hind legs and vomited thick black goo all over me. It melted all of my clothes and started burning my skin. It felt kind of like when you get hot sauce in a cut on your finger, only all over your body. The deer looked down at me and started saying the alphabet, backwards. Then it vanished in a cloud of flies. I was not expecting that. The deer must have had a symbiotic relationship with the flies.

The man scrambled over to his wife. He pulled out a cell phone. Smart cookie, this guy.

He said, after a second of yelling into the phone, "We need to get to the top of the mountain."

I said, "Well, that's pretty doable." I was naked and still burning from the deer's vomit. I rolled around a bit in the dirt. This helped, mostly.

The woman's guts were all spilled out like pasta. The man's hands were covered in blackish-red gunk, from the woman. He was just sobbing and sobbing. He piled all of that stuff back into her! Oh man. It was something. Then he took off his jacket and wrapped it around her middle. Full disclosure: I did not think she was going to make it.

While he was doing all that, I figured I would make a stretcher. This turned out to be just a really good idea. I made it out of an emergency tent that I kept in my backpack. It was a good thing the deer hadn't thrown up and completely melted the backpack. Also at this point I began to notice that my body was covered in runes and lines of raised skin, the lines intersecting and branching out from spokes, and these spokes connected to other spokes so that my entire naked body had on it a whole new set of geometric bones. In addition there were animal skulls: horses, apes, elephants, lizards; I could see them all on or around my nipples. Crap, I thought. It can be pretty hard to explain away some skulls.

I managed to ignore myself and I completed the stretcher, and the man was extremely thankful. I don't really know what letter the lady was working on now. It was sort of consonant-y, like a *k* and *g* back to back, over and over. We needed to get to the road. We walked around the corner, and we could see it.

When we made it to the road, a minivan full of children pulled over. All the kids screamed. The driver, who looked to be their mother, started gagging. Then they all ran away. As we were loading the lady into the car, I saw that they had a This Car Climbed Mt. Impossible bumper sticker. The sticker was obviously brand new, and they hadn't even been to the top yet. Some people, I thought.

I drove the minivan—handled pretty well—up the mountain, where the helicopter was waiting. The sun was out. We unloaded the lady from the back of minivan and brought her to the paramedics. I stood there, naked, and put my hands on my hips. They told the man that because of weight constraints he couldn't come in the helicopter. The helicopter paramedics looked grim. They kept pushing the man back, gently, and he eventually stopped protesting. He was slumped over as they took off. He had just about lain down. I mean, he was ready to call it.

"Hey," I said to the man.

I put my hand on his shoulder. My hand was so many bones. They all shimmered a bit.

"Everything is gonna be okay. And anyway, we're here. Here at the top."

A COLONY OF BATS

by J. Bradley

I flutter my eyelashes in the hopes of getting in her cave.
My father never taught me to stay away from spelunking
metaphors when it came to women.

A SKULK OF FOXES

by Riley Michael Parker

Imagine, if you will, the city of London in 1832. Imagine soot-covered windows, and blackened skies, and streets littered with the corpses of fallen men. Now place yourself there, in this grim English city, up to your hips in filth, just a young woman, age twenty-two, with full red lips, paper-thin skin, and a fading bruise just below your left breast.

In the distance you hear children crying, calling out for death, begging for him to come and relieve them from their torment; a sea of orphans without a reason to mature, without hope for the future, without a full set of teeth between them. You can not see them, have never seen them, but you draw pictures of them on dirty windows, using your index finger to express what you think they might look like. You depress yourself with this, so you draw little triangle ears and whiskers on the orphans and turn them into cats. Mew, mew, mew.

There are men in high places who grow mustaches resembling drowned rats, men who have voices that sound like industry, men who have wives they don't recognize and an unknown number of children, and in the winter, when they'll have you, you entertain them in their chambers and in their places of business, returning to your humble quarters at sunup smelling of pipe smoke and spit, your clothes ripped and stained with shame.

In the houses along the river you will find women who bake their tears into pies, who try and poison the world with their sadness; large, robust women with cunts that resemble luggage and hair as coarse as rope. These women have children the same way that the winter has night, and when they close their eyes they see the future, see the perpetual motion of existence, and thus accept their lives as meaningless. These women were built for sex.

In a small house four doors down from your own wait the foxes, the beasts standing upright like men, dressed in long black coats with top hats and leather gloves, daggers in their paws, whiskey on their breath, and these foxes, they intend to rape you. There are five of them, and some of them will treat you kindly, moving gently, giving you what they think you want, but for the most part they will do the things that you dislike, because that is, in fact, what makes it rape. Wednesday, you can tell, will be the day they get you, but there is no such thing as being prepared. They will circle around you as you walk home from the bars, a fox everywhere you look, and one will whisper "lust," another will say "blood," two of them will touch your hair and you'll kiss the last one on the mouth. And then, of course, they will begin.

AN IMPLAUSIBILITY OF GNU

by Bradley Sands

An implausibility of gnu are crossing Denial. And I'm talking about the river in Egypt, not the psychological defense mechanism. I mean, come on! That would be implausible.

Are you laughing? Did my joke make you laugh? You must be laughing, right?

Shit, you're not laughing.

But don't hold it against me. I couldn't resist. If you were in my flip-flops, you wouldn't have been able to resist either. Now that I've got it out of my system, you don't have to worry about lacking a sense of humor.

So… an implausibility of gnu are crossing the River Denial.

What's that?

You don't know what a gnu is? And you can't be bothered to look it up on Wikipedia?

OK, it's time for me to educate you. Because if there's one

thing I want you to get out of this story, it's an awareness of the power of knowledge.

Gnu is another name for a wildebeest. The word is used interchangeably in a singular and plural form, although I'm using the plural form in the context of this story. Also, you can add an "s" to the end of the plural form if that's your preference.

The English language is an impenetrable beast.

So which team are you on? Team Gnu or Team Wildebeest?

I don't know which word I like better. Wildebeest may be the greatest word in existence, but gnu may be the most enigmatic.

Who would win in a fight: awesomeness or enigmaticness?

Probably enigmaticness because that form of the word does not exist, so it would creep out of the shadows and slaughter the corporeal "awesomeness" word before it got the chance to crack open a dictionary.

Excuse me, I've just been handed a bulletin. It reads, "Actually, the gnu are crossing the psychological defense mechanism, not the river."

Erm, sorry about that.

So… back to the crossing of the psychological defense mechanism—an implausibility of gnu are crossing denial. Some of them get across the psychological defense mechanism unharmed, while others drown or get eaten by crocodiles.

How implausible.

Don't ask me what crocodiles are doing inhabiting denial or how a gnu can possibly drown in a defense mechanism that doesn't consist of water. I don't have the answers. I'm just reporting the facts.

Why are the gnu crossing denial anyway if there is such a high risk of death?

It may have something to do with the video camera equipment they're carrying across the defense mechanism. And how after the survivors reach the other side, they turn around to videotape the deaths of the members of their species. It's like they're shooting footage for a mondo movie like *Faces of Death*.

It's sick. Sick how the gnu who are videotaping from the other side of the defense mechanism have gleeful expressions on their faces as dollar signs materialize over their eyeballs.

I cannot condone profiting off the suffering of others.

So I descend from the heavens and crush the video camera-wielding gnus beneath my size-1000 flip-flops.

I am a vengeful and compassionate god.

And I cannot wait to see my wrath on the Ten O'Clock News.

A COLONY OF BATS

by J. Bradley

Pete's body is a museum of debt: three cracked ribs, right eye a swollen kaleidoscope.

A CROSSING OF ZEBRA

by Jess Dutschmann

Your house was one of the few on your block not razed during the war and stuck out fiercely, an awkward buttermilk tooth against the ashy earth. You were in there, I could tell because the windows were open. I could see your form looking through a back window, hands balled at your sides.

When I knocked at your door: the familiar lock clicked, the sound of Ulysses hitting the door. Change always seemed to suck, and your anger was change. I walked behind calling your name, found you on your back porch watching garbage tumbleweeds whisk across your backyard.

Your dogs were at your ankles like lions guarding a driveway. You nodded, way far across the block, through the remains of neighbors' houses, to a little pond driven black by debris and unearthed coal tar that had erupted from the ground when the area was bombed. I could see dots moving across the road from it, two big and a few little, flea sized from so far away.

You motioned for me to walk with you towards it, so I did, and as we crunched along the dots became animals and then pretty obviously ducks. They were trying to get their babies into the pond, crossing at the crosswalk as though there would be cars, coming out from a big nest in the hollow bit of a hybrid car where someone'd already taken the engine.

"They're all going to die," you said while gesturing to your dogs to heel. As the ducks crossed the road I felt numbness run through my face, down my body.

The ducks walked onto the pond and stood, confused and buoyed by its thick blackness, and the dogs at your feet started snarling. Dogs know bad physics, I think, and it freaked them out so hard that they ran straightaway into the sludge, grabbing the ducks and sinking with them, flapping, blackspray getting everywhere. We didn't move but I saw you quaking.

We crossed to the animals. The dogs crawled weakly out of the pond, holding ducklings like tennis balls in their mouths.

I grabbed a duckling from a mouth, placed it on the ground, and lit its oily skin with a match. I watched it turn from a ball of grease into a small parcel of meat, the down flaming off to reveal pink skin, then picked it up and offered it to you. You turned and threw up, not ready for this level, I guess, so I shoved it in my pocket and headed home.

A SPAN OF MULE

by Andrew Borgstrom

There were questions about the cockfights. About the missing feet. The feet burned toe to heel. Not the cock's feet. And covered in mule fat for a slow and thorough burn.

We brought a hammer to bed, and we asked why and answered no about the fat and the feet.

We made a kind of music with the hammer, a kind of answering. And yes, we sang about the cockfights we knew about.

There were no questions about the expectations. About the reproductions. How one size fits all. And how all sounds represent a sword of chastity placed between the naked bodies of virgin lovers.

We used our hands the way we used our lives. We sang about the things we were born about.

There are many ways to say this but only one way to feel this, which has been said. One mule-gut condom fits all. The bedroom must be heated by another bedroom. The bedroom below must heat its own ceiling out of selfishness and the floor of the bedroom above out of ignorance. The bedroom below must contain baseboard heaters, and the bedrooms together must represent a span of mule.

In between the bedrooms is a ceiling or a floor.

AN AMBUSH OF TIGERS

by Kevin Sampsell

The girl didn't know what kind of club it was until she saw
the transsexual chained to the wall. At first, she didn't know
if it was a real person. It was hard to see in that part of the
room (the first dark left after entering) and the person wasn't
moving. She moved closer and looked at the body, half male
and half female. The breasts were exposed, sloped over a
halter-top that had been yanked down. There were some
tight sparkly shorts unbuttoned below that, but not pulled
down, as if someone became scared of what they might find
tucked in there. The body opened its eyes, surprisingly bright
blue and happy. "What's your name, honey?" the transsexual
said.

The girl jerked her gaze up to the face, the makeup more like
white paint, smooth and flat like a wall. The lips as plump
and red as a tomato. She thought this was maybe a sex doll
and someone was playing a prank. A voice coming through
a hidden speaker in the wall. But the lips moved and the
white teeth glowed from a black light above. She thought of
a policeman's flashlight shining in her eyes. A truly blinding
smile. "Sheila," the girl said.

The body moved now, as if stretching after a nap. "My name is Georgia," the transsexual said. Her hair looked like a Cleopatra wig but it went down to her waist. "Do you like me, Sheila?"

Sheila looked around. She was supposed to meet her friend here in fifteen minutes. She didn't know the name of the place but she was figuring out that it was a sex club. The sign outside just had a heart on it.

"Do you like my tits, Sheila?" Georgia said.

Again, Sheila thought of a hidden speaker saying these words, disembodied and aimed at anyone with the name of Sheila. Maybe it was some kind of electronic trick where they insert your name after you tell them what it is: *Do you like me Sheila, do you like these Sheila, do you like that Sheila, do you like me Sheila, do you like looking at me Sheila, do you like the way I say your name, Sheila?*

"I like them," Sheila said quietly.

"You can touch them," Georgia said. The sound of someone sighing could be heard not far away. Maybe it was Georgia. She could have been sighing and speaking at the same time.

"Why are you chained up?" Sheila asked.

"I'm here every Tuesday," said Georgia. "Don't worry about me. I like you."

Sheila cupped Georgia's breasts with her right hand—one and then the other. Her movements were small and timid. Her left hand stayed stuck shyly to her side.

"Don't just touch them. Feel them," said Georgia.

Sheila traced around them with dragging, nervous fingers.

"Can you give me some money?" whispered Georgia.

Sheila wasn't sure how much money. She had a five and two ones and her credit card. She put the five in the ass pocket of Georgia's shorts. Palm grazing sequins and glitter.

"What kind of tits do you have?" Georgia asked.

Sheila looked down at her chest and realized no one had ever asked her that before. "Just normal girl tits," Sheila said. "Twenty-five-year-old tits."

"Me too, kinda" said Georgia, and then she laughed.

Sheila noticed music getting louder now. The kind of music that some people call "industrial dance."

"Wanna do a bitch huddle?" Georgia said. One of her eyebrows arched.

"What's that?" Sheila asked.

"It's where you press your chest against mine. Come closer. Move my hair out of the way."

Sheila stepped forward and brushed Georgia's long hair aside. It had looked like a dark shawl draped over her shoulders before, but now you could see Georgia's strong arms and shoulders. On both of her upper arms, there were tattoos of tigers—three on each side—looking like they were mid-leap, maybe racing upward to feast on Georgia's neck and face. *Can a tiger eat someone's head?* Sheila wondered now. Her eyes moved back and forth, keeping an eye on the beasts. She wanted to say something about the tattoos, but instead she heard herself ask, "Do you like men or women?"

"I don't think about it that way anymore," Georgia said. "I only like what's inside a person."

"What's inside a person?" Sheila repeated it like a question.

"What's inside a person," Georgia said like an answer.

A COLONY OF BATS

by J. Bradley

You enter the cave. You look up and see bats blanketing the ceiling. What do you do?

To leave the cave, turn to page 113.

To continue on in the cave, turn to page 124.

A LITTER OF PUPS

by Joseph Riippi

In Italy, he said. In the mountains, the pups. They lay about the snow, white and black, half invisible, half-littered, full dead. We'd been ready for children, for mothers and fathers who'd press their small kin to us skiers, pleading, but not knowing the word, the English please. Per favore, American, take, take. We'd ignore, pole ourselves away across their country. Children grow to men, to enemy. Look to your own, we'd shout to the fathers, as though we knew ourselves, our own now so long away gone. But these pups would grow to dogs is all, dogs not knowing nations nor pretense, not knowing either, not knowing even had they been shepherds, which frozen near-fetal maybe they were but who could tell. We stopped in our skis, unslung guns from our backs and lit white cigarettes to birth orange glows that burned in foreignity, lonely things of true color, small dots, the only believability worth looking forward for. We'd given up on going back, on ever seeing something worthy again. And then the pups, littered and motherless, dead and yet somehow worth seeing. One of the boys bent and covered his pup in the snow, gave it a cross over the hump, smoke from his orange. Some other boys repeated, re-repeated, smoke and crosses and none of us speaking, just covering our pups, and then we were slinging guns across shoulders and skiing off again, soldiers in search of whatever mother had left them littered there to die, wanting to bury her too in this war.

A STRING OF PONY

by David Drury

When the Indians killed a buffalo, they used the whole buffalo. What, are you bragging with that? Do you want a cookie? No. You have one. And it tastes like a buffalo.

When Mr. Standish, the butcher, put down Mrs. Prancey-Fance (madness, blindness, phantom kicking), I can't speak to just how much of our family's cherished pony he used in the rendering process, but at least 250 yards of her were wound into the finest pink kite string this side of paradise. String is less insulting than glue, but still. Of little comfort to me was the fact that any Indian would be proud of the strong yet lightweight equine twine. If flying kites was something Indians do, but they don't. At least not that I've seen in any pictures.

How shall I describe it? Pony string is sinewy and rigid, but light like the halo of an angel. Ever wonder about the tough pink skin encircling a baloney? Pony. Reach back and wing a slice of THAT across a school cafeteria. It'll sail on you, man. God did not make anything in a circle like that, by the way. That is a PERSON who made it. From pony. Have you ever heard an expression, "Riding the baloney pony?"

The internet at the church library tells me it means that you have eaten a WHOLE LOT of baloney, so much so that it is akin to being carried away, say, on a literal pony. To my surprise, my sister was a big fan of this manner of baloney consumption, according to close friends and graffiti.

I wouldn't have known anything about Mrs. Prancey-Fance's repurposing, but that I was riding my bicycle on the paved trail at the park a week later. I felt a sudden burning sensation across my neck and was thrown to the ground. Kids were pointing and laughing. I clawed at my throat. I had been clotheslined—with kite string. It was none other than Elmer Standish, son of the butcher who stood clutching that greasy spool of pink string. I was seized with the nearly decapitating truth—pony. Elmer saw the look on my face and swallowed hard. But when the laughs and taunts of the other boys continued, his heart hardened. He flexed his control over my weakness inside this new moment of truth-fueled grief. Elmer began to sneer and delight in the power. He tugged on the string and the kite danced high above us, taunting me, held aloft on dead pony dreams and wind.

I raced home on a mission of revenge. I found my father's hedge clippers and tucked them under one arm. I raced back, salivating when I saw that kite on the horizon, still bobbing above the trees. I made a pass on the paved trail and snipped clean through that string. Elmer and his buddies gasped. The liberated kite shuddered and sailed off across the park, string waving behind it. Elmer and his buddies scrambled onto their bikes and gave chase. And as the kite and her string sailed over the pond, across the road, and down into town, I waved and whispered, "Goodbye Mrs. Prancey-Fance." And I swear that the kite whinnied in response, tossing away sadness with the flick of its mane. And the kite did not float or fly, but only pranced down the avenues on glittery hooves, over rooftops and barns, galloping toward a heaven I had never believed in until now.

A CRASH OF RHINOCEROS

by Jessica Knauss

I was walking along the highway among the freshly leafing poplars. I realized I'd left my keys in the front door. I was thinking I needed a glue to physically attach my necessary items to me when I heard screams and loud, metallic crashing just around the bend.

The eastbound lane was a confusion of cars turned the wrong way, their doors smashed in. Oncoming traffic wended around the mess. The drivers craned their necks to see the damage and stopped, in shock.

In the westbound lane, the majestic bulk of a rhinoceros rose up from the asphalt. He nibbled on grass shoots at the side of the road, his tail swatting at what might have been mosquitoes.

A man in a blue jumpsuit was lurking behind the trees, watching the rhinoceros. "Hello!" I said.

"Shh! I've got to get close to that rhinoceros without him hearing me."

"Are you a professional rhino hunter?" I whispered back.

"No. I'm tracking animals for the city."

He didn't have any obvious equipment about his person.

"Where are your tranquilizer darts? Is your net out for repairs?"

"My net is fine." He whipped a green felt coin purse out of his pocket as if to show me, but put it right back in. It had a chipped gold-tone clasp and decaying rickrack ribbon, as if he had taken it from a pile of forgotten detritus.

He considered me. "It's a busy day—the animals have escaped from the zoo. So I'll be taking my leave." He stared at me, as if to convince me that his work was entirely uninteresting. I turned around, but when I looked back, he was concentrating again, so I watched him at a distance.

When the police cars and ambulances came, he murmured with the officers, urging them to trust him to take care of the rhinoceros. Even as they cleared the wreckage, the rhino grazed unperturbed. The animal catcher extracted what looked like a small bottle of hairspray from his pocket. He crept up behind the rhinoceros and daintily spritzed whatever was in the bottle in the rhino's direction. The catcher waved his hands to encourage the substance to waft onto the rhino's rear. He placed the bottle back into his pocket, took out the coin purse, and stared at the rhino, never taking his eyes from it, although many minutes passed.

Before I realized, the rhino was shrinking, faster all the time. It was the size of a Great Dane, then a Chihuahua puppy, and then I understood why the catcher had to keep such a close watch on the animal. It seemed to disappear altogether. The catcher stooped and picked something up off the ground.

"Hey!" I cried from my hiding place. "What did you do to that beautiful animal?"

He rolled his eyes at me. "It's fine, see?"

I peered into his hand. What looked like an oddly shaped pebble was the rhino, in extreme miniature. He tried to run and charge at the enormous hand. The catcher opened the clasp and slid the rhino inside the coin purse, snapping it shut. I thought I heard an elephant trumpet.

"They're so cute at this size, aren't they?" the catcher said. "It's lucky for them the spray is temporary. Otherwise, I don't know if I could bring myself to give them back to the city."

I imagined a house stacked to the ceilings with tiny wiggling giraffes, puppies, gerbils, and elephants, and realized that people don't need glue to attach them to things. Maybe an opposite polarized magnet to draw them apart.

A COLONY OF BATS

by J. Bradley

You leave the cave, never looking back. You will always wonder what was in that cave. Your marriage will fail because you are hung like regret.

A NURSERY OF RACCOONS

by Tom De Beauchamp

Gertrude is on all fours again, mooing and gagging in
the street. An hour ago we were dancing—do you believe
that?—jitterbugging on the springy floor of the car show. My
suspenders thrummed like bass notes and her skirt hiked up
to her knees. Now she's dumping yellow slime from her liver
into a storm drain in the alley behind our house. It's not the
first time this has happened.

I press my hand for a moment into her back, trying to be
helpful. She has told me, though, that this habit of mine
leaves her feeling like a shelf, and that is not the role she sees
for herself. I have assured her I am no leaner-on of shelves.
Rather, I am her very special lookout. I am her consoler
and her shield. I address for us the world. It is my duty to
scour this dark alley, to remember each dandelion, each
crack in the concrete. I am to record the gentle sway of the
electrical cables. I am to listen for the silence on the other
side of Gertrude's gasping breath. My ears must remain
pricked against all violent possibles: street gangs, coyotes,
photographers, the police.

"Oh, Gerty," I say. "Oh, Gerty Gerty."

From a few blocks away comes the sound of our taxi laying down rubber. The driver no doubt has forgotten us already, forgotten his meager tip, forgotten Gertrude's escalating disrepair, forgotten before he'd even ever remembered. There he is, conflated with roaring of an engine.

And here we are: almost midnight with the new moon lighting nothing, a single street lamp growing from the core of an old, sour plum tree, whose leaves and branches glow orange and almost seem to sparkle. Though the breeze tonight is slight, the tree shivers and thrashes in it, emitting from its heart a chorus of feral yowlings, part catfight, part boiling oil. I breathe deeply and attempt to consume these separate sounds as a single harmonic structure. I want to write down the date and time, the latitude and longitude and call it Opus #1, Plum Tree Plus Taxi Plus Barfing Partner.

Gertrude stands up. Her hair is off a bit, her scalp showing more than it should.

"What are you looking at?" she says and pulls her purse from my shoulder. "I need to brush my teeth," she says, pulling out a napkin.

"How are you feeling?" I ask.

She wipes her lips and wads the napkin into a ball in the palm of her hand. She's obviously shaking tremendously.

"I'm great, Constantine. Thank you." She drops the napkin to the pavement. It lands inches from the neon slick of her bile.

After her fits, Gertrude is always very weak, and walking for her takes great effort. We make a few paces together toward the tree, which is just a few feet from our back yard. She reaches out and grabs my bicep. A shadow drops from the plum, and bolts behind a dumpster.

"I don't care what that was, Constantine," she says, pinching my arm. "Please just take me home."

Within the shadows, behind the leaves, other shadows are breathing. Without a doubt, they're staring at me. Without seeing eyes, I feel eyes, perhaps half a dozen unblinking eyes from the depths of the now silent tree. Like a skirt, the cement around its trunk is smeared with rotten, overripe fruit, and tumbling through the web of its branches, fat as a bear, snout covered in sugary gore and viscera is a tremendous raccoon. As we lock eyes, Gertrude tugs my arm, but she has such little strength.

The big fatty shows me her teeth, flecked with purple skin. I mirror the gesture, growling. How long do we hold our hackles raised? I don't know but something clicks, and we back away slowly. By the time we do, Gertrude is gone.

Up the stairs, the shower is running.

A part of me wants to use the word "terminal" in juvenile, pejorative ways. I calm myself with breathing though and climb the stairs. Gertrude's clothes are laid out on the floor. Her hair is on the desk in a clump, and the blinds are open enough for me to see the streetlight, and the tree.

I pick up her hair and wear it on my fist, its synthetic inner scalp rough on my knuckles. "I'm sorry," I say. "No, seriously," I say, "I'm sorry."

"You're an ass," she says in a diminutive voice.

"I know. I know," I say.

Back in the street three raccoons, the fatty I'd dealt with and her babies, crawl down from the tree. They skitter through the alley in the orange light, their fur almost blonde, the fatty looking left, looking right, and the babies at her side.

A COWARDICE OF CUR
+OR SUBURBAN DOGS+

by Frances E. Dinger

lay down
lay down and wait like
an animal
　　　—Charles Bukowski

When Scout was young, she was a cur and all her siblings
and mother and father were curs as well. They ate out of the
same bowl and her mother taught her and her siblings to get
over their food aggression after one of them had snapped the
neck of a curious kitten and their mother said, "Oh well, oh
well. Oh, dear," before carrying the furry little cat body away
to the trash heap where it composted with banana peels and
egg shells their owners threw out.

She and her siblings would wrestle in the yard but by the
age of six months she was bored of wrestling and in secret
learned to read and practiced standing up on her hind legs
and she nursed complicated unrequited feelings about their
owner's teenage son. In many ways, she had a very typical
childhood though she never felt her age.

Scout lived an exceptionally long time for a dog, 18 years,

but it was just because she was waiting to become something else. Most parents mean it when they tell their children, "Honey, you can grow up to be whatever you want."

After she was done being an old dog, she became a young woman. When the last of her dog teeth fell out, she lay in bed sleeping for an entire day and when she woke up she had bald toes on her feet and a thumb on each hand. She felt longer than she had been before and she stretched, finding herself too big for the dog bed. She put on some clothes and slightly chewed boots she had been saving, leaving the house while her people were at work.

She spent her first day as a woman sitting in a cafeteria style diner, slowly reading a newspaper. After she asked for her fifth refill on coffee, the waitress (who kind of just wanted her to leave because she wasn't buying anything but coffee and a couple pieces of wheat toast with peanut butter) asked for Scout's name.

"Scout. That's a dog's name," the waitress said.

"Yeah," Scout said. So she changed her name to a person's name but she didn't know what normal people called themselves so she named herself after the first thing she saw, which happened to be a sign advertising "Vacancies at AVA CONDOS." She knew enough about the names of people to know that people did not spell their names in all capital letters so she was, "Ava." Her husband Tom later said she should have named herself something soft and abnormal like "Windy." He said she could still change her name if she wanted because not very many people knew her and even humans who were born human changed their names sometimes. But Ava stayed Ava. She was tired of changing and she worried if she willed herself to be "Windy," she would have less mass and might float away. She had a need to feel anchored, weighed down, so she married Tom after five months of being human.

Tom liked to tell people at parties that Ava hadn't owned a pair of shoes until she married him. Tom also liked to tell people he and Ava had met at a dog park. Neither assertion was true. Tom could sometimes be mean but sometimes Ava could be an animal, so it all evened out eventually. When they fought, Ava gnashed her teeth and growled and her nostrils flared but she could no longer bark without feeling silly so she screamed. Tom would sometimes hide in the bedroom until his mongrel-wife calmed down. Eventually, he would feel safe enough to come out and would sear some tofu for dinner or make her a martini. She was a savage when she was younger, but she stopped eating meat a long time ago. She took her tea with lemon and lots of honey. She was a compulsive eater when she was stressed. She never slept for more than six hours at a time. Her sense of smell rivaled anyone around, which would have made her a good detective, but instead she mostly stayed inside and cultivated human skills like laughing and speaking at an appropriate volume.

When Tom returned home from work, Ava tried out lines on him. When he sat silent at dinner, she would ask "What are you thinking?" She had maybe heard that phrase spoken at a high volume on a video cassette her former humans watched once. She liked that the "about" was implied. English has a lot more implications and subtleties than the dialect of dogs. "What are you thinking?" seemed like a very Hollywood phrase.

(Or maybe the video cassette people said, "What were you thinking?" in an accusatory tone. It took Ava awhile to understand the significance of tenses.)

"What are you thinking?" "What were you thinking?" She tried both and got the same result.

When she was bored with movies, she studied maps, memorizing state and country and capital names. She would take herself for walks around the city reciting place names under her breath, trying to recall the image of the map in her head, or else she would go after a scent and end up someplace where they were smoking fish or in front of a hotdog vendor, salivating but never ordering. One day a man just gave her a tofu hotdog and she was so happy she got lost on her way home and had to call Tom on her cell phone. On the drive back, they kept the windows rolled up. Tom had the good taste not to joke about leashes. She complained about feeling sick from eating the hotdog, so Tom let her lie on the couch while he rubbed her belly.

A few weeks later, she got lost a second and third time and Tom decided they couldn't live in the city. They bought a house in the suburbs with a big backyard. The first night after they moved in, they did victory laps running in circles in the yard before collapsing into the grass, tongues lolling. The bed hadn't been set up yet, so they spent the first night on the floor. When it was morning, Ava brought the newspaper into the kitchen where Tom was making coffee and toast. He gave her a new necklace just because and showed her how to work the thermostat before he left for work.

Ava spent most of her time alone in the yard and slowly began to talk less at dinner. There wasn't really anywhere to walk anymore but sometimes she and Tom would drive into town for vanilla ice cream cones. They never talked about getting a dog or kids.

For her birthday in the fall, Tom built her a gazebo in the center of the grass. Her own island, her own room. "A room of your own, my Virginia Wolf." She ignored the ironic emphasis on "wolf." She hadn't yelled at him in a long time. Tom poked her ribs when he came inside to ask for water but she didn't squirm or push him away. She started sleeping a lot and got a little fat.

"You are arriving into your humanity," Tom said.

"What?"

"Oh, nothing."

The next summer, a burglar broke into their neighbor's house and stole some expensive electronics and some jewelry. When the police came, one officer said quietly to the neighbor's wife, "Have her check her underwear drawer." Nothing was taken from there, though. Which was good because she said that would have really freaked her out, the neighbor woman.

For the rest of the summer, Ava spent the afternoons reading and listening to the radio in the gazebo. She avoided the interior of the house until her husband returned from work.

Suburban dogs and women are experts in stranger danger but she wasn't afraid of getting raped or killed. She knew she could be an animal. If a burglar entered the house, she would not be able to call the cops. If a burglar entered the house, she would immediately be at his throat and they say once a dog has the taste of blood in her mouth, it will never get out. She was afraid of what they do to animals once they lose control. She had heard they do far worse things to people. She imagined Tom coming home from work, a dead man laid on the doormat like the gift of a bird or squirrel. She would be in the bathroom brushing her teeth and spitting profusely. Tom would stand in the doorway in horror, suddenly aware of what the commitment he'd made to her meant. She would repeat, "This is all for you, this is all for you," which is all any bad dog ever wants to say.

A sad dog howled somewhere down the block and it kept howling for several minutes. It was the only sound Ava could hear. She sat with her knees to her chest in the gazebo and put her hands over her bald ears.

A COLONY OF BATS

by J. Bradley

You walk through the cave. When you trip on a rock, the blanket tucks you in. You will not wake up.

A SNEAK OF WEASEL

by Maurice Burford

The drink only got to me when I was weary, when I was blood-sick. My legs felt it first. Then it would travel up into my gut and hang there, silent and warm.

If I hit her, it was only on account of being blood-sick.

And, of course, I always did hit her.

When I wake up it is crisp out, the smell of damp wood and shit. Outside, the ground crackles as a car moves away. The sun humming against the hollows of my face, I get up off the floor and begin to take stock of my errors. Gulls have come in the window. They are spread out across the room. Maybe a dozen of them. There is one pecking at the face of her. There is one on the lamp with its eye gone—a black hole the size of a button. I also feel there is one standing on the back of my leg, myself kneeling now, looking out the open window and wishing against the strong drink and my not having closed the fucking window.

This time something has broken in her that can not be mended. This was the woman who darned my socks. I watched her drink milk, and had called her a cunt. I once pushed her into Penobscot Lake. I made her drink the water before she could come back up.

A RAG OF COLTS

by Suzanne Burns

Teresa believed dousing homeless people with spare change and baking brownies for her elderly aunt would beatify her enough to be remembered.

She wasn't searching for heaven and was not particularly religious beyond flinching when people said "Goddamn" in front of her, usually at a barbecue where baked beans were somehow involved.

"And Richard Ramirez can go Goddamn fuck himself," her father told Teresa, if she kept sending him letters in jail.

"Don't you know why they call him The Night Stalker? It isn't even half as romantic as it sounds," her mother added, of course at a barbecue, as the juice of baked beans pooled around her mouth like something sticky and X-rated.

"That's why I'm changing my address before your next invitation," Teresa mumbled to herself after the party as she rinsed and dried her potato salad bowl and placed it high in a kitchen cupboard next to her rag of colts.

The rag, a yellowed handkerchief rimmed in cornflowers, frayed from concealing the weight of three pistols. Inherited from an uncle, she called the Colt 45's her ponies as she imagined them jockeying for position inside the mildewed kerchief. Teresa knew everyone frowned at the idea of saints shooting guns, or even fondling bullets, but once she decided to hide each gun inside a cake, of course homemade, she began calling herself St. Teresa, even in her dreams.

St. Teresa of the Incarcerated, she spent an entire afternoon baking cakes. One chocolate, two lemon creams and a vanilla Bundt. The trick to hiding a Colt inside each confection revolved around the frosting. Skillfully twirled buttercream rosettes concealed every bump and ridge, but when Teresa closed her eyes at the end of the day, she heard a stable of possibilities galloping beneath.

No matter how lonely hearted, no one could visit The Night Stalker, and Teresa lived nowhere near California. Plus he had never responded to even one of her dozen letters, but the fantasy of a man knowing just what to say to get close enough to kill you compelled Teresa to find a new paramour.

Calls to two correctional facilities near her home resulted in Teresa's plan ending before its true conception. Strangers cannot give prisoners any gifts. There are metal detectors. And Type 2 diabetics. And it is easy to hide undesirable things inside of layer cake, ma'am, everyone knows that.

So St. Teresa of the Unwanted Confections tucked her kerchief into her jeans pocket and borrowed a little red wagon from a neighbor boy. She wheeled her cakes towards the center of town. She went at night. She wore perfume and that color of lipstick that never gets lost in translation. She even stuck a sign in each cake, three little flags with the word "Free" scrolled in red ink.

But no men came. No new Night Stalkers. A few walked by her, some even stopped to smell the air, musky and floral near her neck. But not one man had the intuition to see a gun beneath the lemon and chocolate layers.

Teresa then stared at the women. The kind of women out late at night, standing where she stood with the same unapologetic lipstick, were lucky the Night Stalker was sitting in a cell far away and that they had no time to write him because they always slept in.

Teresa picked up a lemon cake and handed it to the closest blonde.

"Fuck you!" she responded, and knocked the cake from St. Teresa of the Underappreciated Hands.

A gun revealed itself among the yellow crumbs. St. Teresa of the Disenchanted picked up the gun and pointed it at the woman. She wanted to scare her into accepting another cake, into accepting that possibility hides in the most unexpected places.

The woman grabbed for the chocolate cake and shoved as much as she could into her mouth. So much she choked a little. This made St. Teresa of the Bruised Esophagus smile. She smiled more when the woman, who kept swallowing cake, found a gun among the dark frosting and pointed it at her.

St. Teresa of the Stand-Off moved closer to the woman,

closer to the possibility of being something close to holy. She unfolded her kerchief with the faded cornflowers, ready to catch any spilled blood, because sainthood always involves bruising. St. Teresa of the Last Dying Breath fell to the ground, unable to move or remember who shot first as she felt blood pool in the corner of her mouth. She smiled as the rag in her hand turned red, as the Colts continued to jockey for position on the ground next to her, as she waited for a halo, tarnished or pristine, to float above her head.

+A+
+TOWER+
+OF+
+GIRAFFE+
++

A TOWER OF GIRAFFE

by Hazel Cummings

In the basement find children, dirty and malnourished
but pleased, not happy by any means but amused with
themselves, wearing plastic pig masks and rags sewn into
something resembling clothing. These children have knives
and hatchets and lead pipes
and
so
much
patience.
They will wait as long as it takes.
All they want to do is eat and eat (and eat, and eat, and eat,
and eat) and eat and eat and eat and eat.

On the ground floor find children, clean, well-groomed,
wearing slick fur coats and pilot caps with pointy little ears
fixed on the top. These children spend their days eating,
sleeping, ignoring the help, licking themselves and each
other, chasing mice and balls of yarn. The girls go into heat
every three or four weeks, backing themselves up to anything
and everything, but the boys have all been fixed, and this
is a good thing, because their penises are barbed and their
stamina is great.

If only the girls knew what they were missing out on they would be grateful instead of bitter, but as it stands now they thrash and scratch and attack strangers, reaching out from underneath the couches and coffee tables to claw the legs of passersby, all of them filled with a confusing and all-consuming lust.

In the upper floors of the northern wing find children, dusty, statuesque, wearing capes like wings and caps with feathers poking out like long antenna. These children are children of the light, but not the sun, they hate the sun, adore only the unnatural glow of electricity through bulbs of glass, the children always hiding during the day, tucked away in coat closets, sustaining their bodies on shirts and trousers and underwear, coming out at night to circle around a lamp and read to each other from whatever books that may have been left out. They know that they know nothing of the world, and they love it.

In the attic attached to the eastern wing find children, lots and lots of blind little children, small, ferocious, snub-nosed big-toothed inbred children, all of them dressed in brown corduroy pants, white button-up shirts, and black leather vests, their hair fixed with hairspray into cones that resemble horns. Some of these children eat bugs, some of them eat fruit, some of them drink blood, but all of them are pests, and when given a chance outsiders have been known to beat the children to death with brooms, or to light them on fire, or to shoot them with 22's.
These children deserve all of this and more.

In the tower to the south of the property find children, thin, healthy, proud, with large eyes surrounded by big beautiful lashes, with tongues that they are always sticking

out, sometimes to flirt, other times to cause offense. These children are always dressed in the same elaborate patterns, obsessed with fashion but all longing to be like one another, wanting to stand out and blend in all at once. These children walk on stilts to entertain themselves, strut around to entertain each other, and take turns reaching out from the tower windows to grab the fruit that no one else can get to. They may seem calm and graceful, but when threatened these children have been known to kick others to death, with the stilts and without, in a matter of moments.
As much as possible, avoid the tower.

As much as possible, avoid this house.

A TOWER OF GIRAFFE

by Ted Powers

We're sitting in a bar. I want the night to last longer. A day passes. What do I do with my problem, I say to you on a beach. Lock it in the shed until it starves to death, you say. You get up and wipe the sand off your ass and leave. My skin feels like a tent with a broken zipper. I take a sip of the coffee you left behind. I tell myself things are okay. Then a giraffe walks out of the ocean.

It follows me home. It stares into my bedroom. It eats fruit through the broken window. I lead it toward the shed. Behind the giraffe is another giraffe who pulls up next to it. There are more giraffes behind them and more are coming. Soon my yard is filled with long legs and bodies and necks. By the shed, I can't see the sky, I can only see giraffe.

As they fight for space in my small yard, many are trampled. Blood gets on hooves and the cartilage of horns. A giraffe coughs up yards of tongue onto the back of another giraffe. What I think is you is just the space between a giraffe and its insides.

A TOWER OF GIRAFFE

by Lauren Tamraz

Swahili class met Mondays and Wednesdays, and after a few weeks they stopped wearing shoes when they went there. The world became an extension of their home: this brick walkway, this bench glazed in green paint, this laughing sky all were soaked up by their lives. Soft soles walked into the classroom.

When the semester began, sunsets were enjoyed after class, a ritual like the viewing at a wake: yes, this day happened, and I know it because I saw its end. Eventually their tongues stumbled less over clashing consonants, and sunsets began to intersect class time. Their professor explained how in Mombasa the day begins and ends on the sixes because it is equatorial country, and this is when the sun reveals and retracts itself.

One warm afternoon they arrived at class to find a note on the door:
Wanafunzi,
Siku ni kubwa mno. Kuwa nje.
Kwa upendo,
Mwalimu

Their teacher had used simple words and the students understood his message, urging them to recognize the day's beauty and take a break. From his stories they knew midday naps and birthday parties attended by the whole town were all a part of small-town Mombasa charm. Today's lesson was not being postponed, it was practicing cultural immersion.

They drove west out of town toward the large hills. The sun would not set for an hour. In the backseats of their cars, some had special items in case of emergency: climbing gear, hand drums, LSD.

They parked on the side of the road. Some had put on shoes. Some were watching the sun with their eyes closed. Walking single file down the deer trail into the woods, the light lagged behind them in the pines and mountain laurel. The air smelled of juniper and someone said it was the anniversary of her brother's death. She said he died just like a lion; one of them asked later what that meant and she said: with lots of sound.

The trail was covered in leaf mold. It dipped down an embankment and ended at a deep well in the river. The river ran swiftly across the limestone, but the giant well loomed enormous and iced tea-colored before allowing the stream to continue on past it.

One by one they stripped off excess layers, some removing all their clothing entirely. Mountain fed, the water bit at their white cheeks and stained breasts a rose color beneath the clear surface. Salamanders rushed to hide in rock crevices from their land-born feet.

Many flat slabs of stone lay on the banks. The boys shared

the burden of stacking them in the water. They pressed them as simply as they could, thinking first of their backs and then of stability.

The girls treaded the river like goats at solstice; their slick heads bobbed and their chests were wet and lovely as they sank and re-emerged. The boys carried the smallest girl and placed her at the foot of their rock pile. Naked, she carried an armful of rocks like a baby to her chest, and when she reached the top of the pile she threw them down to smash and clatter hollow and satisfying like fresh broken sticks of chalk.

The boys gathered in the water as the other girls climbed out, dripping. They gathered dusty armfuls to scatter and looked like dancing seals in the low afternoon light, reduced to silhouettes only. Their sound was the rhythm of bodies tearing from water, wet toes on hot rock, stones falling from arms and repeating again.

Hot, dry rocks became scarce as they all sunk into the river's depression. Girls hunted the banks for more and the rhythm slowed. One boy left the river and lifted a girl, ascended the rocks.

He dropped her and waited for the sound that so many of the rocks had made. The sun could not be seen any longer and they observed the rules of Mombasa. The girls fell like sticks of chalk and the boys tried to recall the ways to translate.

A TOWER OF GIRAFFE

by Jess Rowan

+
+

The spot was more like an itch than an echo. We stood on the spot, pumping it full. We massaged the wits into it.

When it took a breath, we also took to breathing.

We thought to build a home of it, but could not conclude a method of building without the obscenity of rafters. The spot used pressure points to agree to this.

+

The spot began to be filled in other ways. The feet of others left glitter and paste. The paper collected during the third year, all the promises of a generation too big for animals.

I am a builder of animal parcels, one said. They are much more efficient.

Those mornings we began to rush to the spot. We began to lose our delicate nature.

+

The first giraffe was born at such a distance we could have scooped it in a firm palm. As we got closer only the pile grew, the mess of soaking legs remaining just matchsticks in a bowl.

+
+

A TOWER OF GIRAFFE

by Peter Schwartz

I'm on a safari inside the worst parts of my heart. I'm making bad decisions. Writing this is a bad decision. The jungle smells permanently wet. My feet have a fungus in the shape of Africa. I've got to keep moving though. I'm hunting for giraffe. I've found five of their droppings since last Wednesday. They make me want to shit myself, but I have no food. There's nothing going through me. I've got to keep moving.

Their tracks are holes made by unsure feet. They're doubling up on themselves. Their ghosts are telling me to leave them alone, but I'm really this much of an asshole. I'm going to break one's neck and slice her open and roast the meat over an open fire with nobody watching (maybe even because no one is watching). I'm going to kill the most beautiful thing in my life. It's not religious or anything, it's just something to do.

I'll blame them for being all neck, for being so grotesquely vulnerable in a jungle like this. I'll complain that the meat's a bit gamey as I pick it out of my teeth. I'll tell myself neither of us have ever existed when it's time. I'll wrap my cold, wet feet in the hide after cleaning it wrong. I'll have blood on my feet and for a while it will make prints on the ground. Then I'll tear everything off and just run like a giraffe.

+CREATURES+
+OF+
+THE+
+SEA+
++

A SMACK OF JELLYFISH

by Stephen Tully Dierks

A Fictional Version of My Ex-Girlfriend As I Imagine Her
In Her Teenage Years pictures being inside waves: a weight
shoving her scrawny limbs down toward the packed sand
and shells. The nerve endings in her scalp tingling.

She walks past lines of blankets and umbrellas alongside
A Fictional Version of Her Dad. On her silver one-piece
bathing suit, a spiral of stars in every color of the rainbow,
each smaller than the next. Her pink sandals hit her heels
flap flap flap. A Fictional Version of Her Dad wears dark blue
trunks and no shirt, his eyes barely visible behind wrap-
around sunglasses.

They had parked on the bluff. From that altitude, everyone
on the beach and in the water appeared to be colorful
abstractions.

A Fictional Version of Her Dad removes the towel from
across his broad shoulders with one hand and tosses it over
A Fictional Version of My Ex-Girlfriend As I Imagine Her In
Her Teenage Years's head. "You ready to swim?"

She shakes her head no, takes the towel off her head and discards it on his chest.

"You told your mother you wanted to go swimming."

They find an empty place for their towels a few feet from the shallows where A Vaguely Metaphorical Boy uses a stick to write his name in the wet sand.

"Do you want to build a sandcastle?"

A Fictional Version of My Ex-Girlfriend As I Imagine Her in Her Teenage Years sits at the foot of her blanket. She hunches over, her small shoulders creating shadows on the sand. The Vaguely Metaphorical Boy lies down in the shallows until the water soaks over him and his name. He springs to his feet and runs away.

When they lived on Ocean Drive, A Fictional Version of My Ex-Girlfriend As I Imagine Her in Her Teenage Years used to play hide-and-go-seek with The Metaphorical Neighbor Boy. The Metaphorical Neighbor Boy had curly blonde hair and pointy teeth. A Fictional Version of My Ex-Girlfriend As I Imagine Her in Her Teenage Years forced him to play by her rules, because A Fictional Version of Her Mom had seen him hogging the ball once and told her not to put up with that. So she kept the ball most of the time, and he chased her around the yard like a dog after food.

When they were tired of that, they climbed into the little plastic wading pool. They couldn't both fit, so each allowed one leg to dangle over the side. That was when they were happiest, when they stopped chasing each other and sat in the water. They traced their little fingers in it and picked out the specks of dirt. They looked at themselves in it and resisted the urge to dunk the other's head. Afterwards he'd blurt something and dash through the hole in the fence back to his yard. When A Fictional Version of Her Mom and A Fictional Version of Her Dad got back, they told her Dad was moving out.

A Fictional Version of My Ex-Girlfriend As I Imagine Her in Her Teenage Years doesn't want to get in the water.

"I'm not getting in."

A DOSE OF CRABS
+THE TALK+

by Ben Tanzer

"It's just a dose of crabs," the doctor said to me, "that's all, don't worry, we can fix that."

What I want to do is stop thinking about the crabs. How I got them. What I had to do to rid myself of them. How all this ties into being the kind of father I want to be. Or more accurately, how all this leads back to my father, which I suppose still ultimately ties into the kind of father I want to be.

This is not the time to lose myself in this reverie, however.

Nor is it the time to think about how my father wanted to ensure he played a role in orchestrating my first sexual experience. How it didn't matter to him whether I was ready or not.

Again though, what I need to do is focus on the task at hand, and I need to focus on my son and the talk and why we even have to have the talk in the first place.

How I walked into his room looking for my laptop and

found him, his dick in one hand, my laptop in the other, some woman's ass shaking across the screen. How he smiled at me, closed the laptop, pulled-up his sweat pants and left the room. How there is now a chasm of silence between us. Not anger or disappointment, but a space that needs to be filled, and tended to, a space that I will fill and tend to by being what my father could not; a listener, a purveyor of information and someone attuned to how difficult and confusing the emergence of one's sexuality can be.

My dad was not that. He was fine, but we didn't talk about things. Things were. Life was. You figured it out. Or you didn't, and if you didn't, you didn't think about it anymore.

And so it was that he took me to see the part-time bookkeeper from his office that did other things on the side to make rent.

How he knew this about her I didn't ask. I asked why though, and he said that it was his job to ensure I became a man. It was all that really mattered.

Today we can't do that. Or maybe we just don't. But that's okay, I don't want to. I will talk to my son about the mechanics. How things work, the science. I will tell him that there is pleasure involved, but responsibility as well, both to himself, and to the girls, or boys, he will have sex with.

I can do that, and I will do that.

My son might ask me though about my first time. Or what my father and I discussed. My father is long dead now and my son is always interested in how my father did things, my father being the model for his own father, a father he doesn't always understand.

What will I say? That I was scared, but wanted to be cool so my father wouldn't be embarrassed for him, or me? That the bookkeeper smelled like the ocean, like a breeze that slowly washed over and then engulfed me? Or, that she took it slow and didn't laugh at my fumbling efforts to enter her?

Maybe I should mention how soft she was to the touch, in mostly good ways, but also in ways that seemed different than the girls my age who had let me feel them up? I could tell him about how fast I came, that it was all a blur and a tangle, and that it was done, just like that, a moment of warmth and joy, a shudder, and then over, definitely something great, but over quickly, and only to get better, later.

I could tell him how the next day when my hand shifted below my belt there was no laptop, but there was her feel and smell, the memory of her enough alone, and wonderful all by itself, if not for the sudden itch I felt, if not for the dose of crabs she had left me as a parting gift.

I could also tell him how to this day I cannot jerk-off without unconsciously scratching myself first. It would be funny, private, something he and I can share, but will he even want to hear any of this? Will he want to talk at all?

We'll see.

A SWARM OF EELS

by Jim Ruland

The sea horses were the first to go. A whole herd—three battalions worth—wiped out in an instant. They were corralled in the kelp forest, tied up to the stocks of lost anchors that had settled into the depths and now protruded from the luminous green, like iron grave markers. When the blast came, those poor horses melted inside their armor until their bones and liquefied flesh spurted out of their ruptured eye sockets. They never had a chance. We sent in a scabbard of swordfish from the Deepwater Elite Reconnaissance Patrol. But they fared no better against the O.G.'s terrible new weapon. A single nuclear harpoon was all it took. Its destructive force snapped their spines, sheared off their fins, flayed them to pieces. A thousand cooked carcasses rose to the surface. The scavenger birds came swarming out of the sky and feasted on the stinking island of meat. Our casualties were enormous. Dolphin commandos, jellyfish rangers and tiger shark shooters were obliterated before they could join the battle. Our ground forces, legions of lobsters, crabs, mollusks and sea spiders carpeted the bottoms, their shells fused with the reefs in which they hid. We could hear their screams as we retreated from the front lines for the safety of the cold depths. We were all so fucking scared.

de camp in a dark trench and ate our earth rations,
ring what to do. Why did they want to wipe us
Where did they get those harpoons? We were not so
rent. The O.G.'s were made in our image to serve us and
serve us. Tricky little shrimp with nothing better to do
an swim the sun-warmed shallows. Prolonged periods of
inactivation made us docile. It was bred into us so that we
were slow to wake up to the truth: the O.G.'s were selling
off our cysts as fish food. After the long sleep, after being
hydrated and hatched, some discovered they'd been sold into
slavery for the purpose of entertaining children. Once we
ruled the seas. Or thought we did. Now the Ocean Gorillas
laid claim to the raging main and all its domains. It wasn't
supposed to be like this.

In the morning came the news that Electric Company had
survived the blast. We expected them to limp back to base
and retreat to their pits, but they returned energized and full
of fight. They'd somehow absorbed the destructive energies
of the O.G.'s weapon and were ready to use it against them.
Squadrons regrouped and reformed. Battle plans were
drawn up. Rumors electrified the camp. Some worried about
radiation. Some worried about algae and diatoms. Some
worried that we weren't worried enough. The decision was
made to launch a new offensive to show those gorillas who
the real monkeys were. We sent in swarms of morays, and
when the O.G.'s unleashed their wonder weapons on us
Electric Company retaliated with wave after wave of eels.
We made the seas boil with blood and radiation until every
last one of those aquarium scum was put into permanent
hibernation, a stasis so prolonged, a sleep so severe, their
whole misbegotten race will live and die forever inside its
own endless dream.

A FRENZY OF SHARKS

by Matt Ferner

Not that kind. And not these sharks. Not those. These sharks.
The sharks. Sharks. Shark sharks. Sharks with suits in suits
that drape themselves over their shark pack, laughing deep
in the gut like too lazy to really laugh or too full or too filled
with hate and too drained of goodwill in late afternoon, post-
meal slow sludge, post-loss, post-positive, post-possible,
post-post, post-meaning, post-post-meaning, post-body,
post-life, post-the sound a shark makes before he violates,
enters a life uninvited, forcibly and violently. Or passes out,
post-pass-out sound. Or take card sharks, those were post-
sharks and they even had a shark that made them keep their
shark instincts sleeved or holstered or finned or whatever it
is that a shark, even of cards, does when they have to stalk
and keep to themselves and feel empty in their insides and
hazy in their brains like there is no protein in the life fluid
and life flesh, like they just want to connect with something
or anything or nothing, not anything. And devour it. Whole.
Rip it. And/or bite it. And/or drown it. And/or bleed it and
bring it to the bottom of the ocean where there is nothing
but hot and dark and cold and invisible fish that die when
light splashes on them, or when the pressure is too low they
explode due to a lack thereof the wherewithal of which

for which there which is no pressure. Like a blood vessel pre-burst, thick and juicy and dark and oozy and a secret growing that can be traded amongst those sharks that understand the marketplace, exacting cold and dark and pressured. Filled with purpose and meaning and can roll up its sleeves when the day is rough and throw its thing around the shoulders and desperately feel connected and together yet so alone and dark and cold and filled with the pressure. The pressure attracts the sharks together, they want the pressure to feel it, to sit still and feel it push out on their skin and their brains and skulls and push in on their skin and their brains and their skulls. Or the ache. Or when the shark, the frenzy begins and that sound can be felt, goes too deep and filled with pressure that it's not really heard, it's felt, it tingles. The sound, it makes the frenzy, it conjures it and it begins and the pressure is let out onto the thing or the things and the other sounds that fill the darkness in sleep when we are children and don't know where we are even though we are just several feet from our houses or when we look at our fathers and they don't know what the pressure is either and why it calls us to feel it and release it and push it out onto other things and make that thing feel everything all at once. Ah, but pressure, now that's what makes the shark a shark's shark. A shark that other sharks hate or love or want to make that guttural sound at or to, sounds that sound like joy got its leg caught between two rocks that a jackhammer is pounding pounding pounding. Or that dull tear of flesh that feels so satisfying to hear, like it awakens a reptilian inside that remembers what it felt like to tear into flesh, spill guts, bathe in life matter and watch it drain and then go back to hating and being alone and banging rocks into rocks into rocks until a shape of something so frustrating comes out of that rock and fingers are smashed and the brain cannot concentrate on more than one thing. Or take shark fin soup. It's delicious. But a shark would never tell you that, it would be considered a weakness, the enjoyment of something suggests warmth or relation or common ancestry or that there may just be a right and a wrong after all, that the sharks don't really know what is what from what, but that they are just as cold and dead and filled with pressure and feeling the pressure that we do, but don't know how to hide. The shark knows how to hide. And the movie about the one shark that does that thing that sharks do sometimes and the surfer who got the thing bit off and/or chewed and/or bled and/or entered forcibly, violently. And the shark week on television showing television blood and television sharks with sunglasses dead eyes and contractual obligations that mean more pressure to deliver upon the promise of pressure relieved and pushed out onto the things with the shark pack and the knowing glances and the one that lies on the bed drugged or innocent or wanting to just be part of the shark pack while the sharks loosen their ties and trousers and get ready to enter together to feel the pressure on them and then let it out. There are more sharks. Sometimes even more than that. And there are far more dead sharks than there are alive, but the living ones remember the dead ones in their shape and their weird way they can't look at eyes directly or are terrific at sports or know how to calculate with gaussian copula or the way they want to talk about other sharks and what they would do to them with them while other sharks watched or later did the same thing only because of the things that happened to dead sharks.

+

+AN+
+ABOMINATION+
+OF+
+PLATYPUS+
++

+

AN ABOMINATION OF PLATYPUS

by Crispin Best

From the couch I can do anything. I can jump and land on my face. I have my phone and I can make anything happen.

I want to be in the high parts of my flat. I got halfway up the bookcase and one of the shelves tipped over and down I went and lay there covered in books.

It's OK. I'm going to phone you now.

I moved bottles off the top of the fridge so I could sit up here and call you, but now I'm just drinking what was in the bottles and looking at my phone.

On the swivel chair I can hold on to the ceiling fan and spin. Then I can let go and lean forward and fall. I'm not sure what bones I want to break exactly. For example, my ribs. Do I want to break my neck? I should think about that.

I am on my filing cabinet and I have the phone in my hand. I'm bouncing my heels off the metal. Can I time it so that my face will hit the floor between you picking up and you saying hello? I think you'll say hello three times and then you'll just hang up.

I've decided: Every month you don't have a period I am going to draw a face on an egg and post it through your front door. Then I'll come home and sit on the clothes horse and think of you in your bed, your body curled around the egg to keep it warm.

When I order a pizza, the delivery man lets himself in and walks over to the table I'm standing on. We swap the pizza for the money. When he drives away I open the box and put my face on the pizza and sleep.

I lost a lot of money playing roulette online while sitting on the chest freezer just now. I need money. I am going to make money somehow. Is it easy?

I've been thinking about biting my fingers off since a few hours after you finished baking that cake. The only number on this phone is yours.

I've decided: I think I'm going to be brave. I'm going to do it. I'm going to leave the house and come give you this egg.

The curtain rail fell down. I shouldn't have even tried.

I was just thinking about the last time I kissed you, but I'm not sure, because in the memory our mouths are full of dry leaves.

You hardly leave your house either. That is one of the reasons I'm here now on the table. Yeah. I'm going to lie on this table awhile.

How do people make money? I think I'm going to listen to Wagner and write advertising copy for a teeth whitening product. Can I make money doing that? I think you'll know. If I'm still conscious after my head hits the floor, I'll try to remember to ask.

From the table I can see every wall in this room. How do I choose which one to head butt on the way down? I'm imagining some kind of harness that lets me hit all four.

When you came round, I stood on the swivel chair. I watched you until you wanted the whisk. I wheeled myself over and looked in the drawer. We were quiet. I touched a peeler and said,
"Peeler."
And I touched a grater and said,
"Grater."
And I gave you the whisk and said,
"Whisker".

And I went over and lay face down on the couch and said words into a cushion I found there.

I wanted to be on top of the boiler instead of the couch. I wanted you to stop baking so I said,
"Come lie on me." But you didn't, and you finished the cake and you said you felt sick and you left.

I woke up on the dresser last night and I thought someone was breaking in, but the door was locked. But then I thought about death anyway so I had to jump up on the countertop and try to be quiet. It was funny being up there naked. My bum touched the kettle and it was cold until finally I was OK.

The cake is in a tin somewhere. I don't remember. I'll ask you if I have time before you hang up.
I didn't fit in the cupboard, even after I took everything out. I will never need this many bowls. I put my phone in a bowl, and then in another bowl, and now I'm holding it again.

I'm going to lie here on the countertop and then I might phone you. I'll be a while. I'll be here as long as my phone battery lasts.

AN ABOMINATION OF PLATYPUS

by Chelsea Laine Wells

The child will not die. He lies boneless, seething a foul yellow heat, his eyes flat black like burned coins. They seem to always be open. His lips are cracked and dead white but he needs something more substantial than water; she would open a vein and bleed down his throat if her blood wasn't poisoned. She drags herself to the bed and leans over his face and cries. Please die, she begs him, please let go. He shakes convulsively, rattling the headboard like a lover. She crawls across the gritty carpet and slumps into a corner and holds the glass pipe up to the weak ceiling light. There is nothing left but she smokes it anyway and sleeps with her head on her arms and her legs hunched under herself like a child hiding. She dreams about thick slabs of mold, pale and clotted as the back of a sick tongue, furling open inside the room like a rain mushroom. It rushes up the walls with a sound soft as the separation of a kiss. She wakes hours later and drifts into the bathroom without looking at the child. In the bathroom she drinks water from her cupped hand and takes out the tiny baggie to count the crystals inside, then tucks it away. She orbits to the window, the door, the bed. The boy drags down each breath as though around some dreadful barrier; perhaps the inside of his chest has ruptured

and broken like the ribs of a sinking ship. She closes her eyes
and whispers mercy peace silence, mercy peace silence.

She found him a month ago at a truck stop where she
stopped to buy cigarettes. He was shirtless and his shoulders
folded in towards his chest like the wings of a cold bird.
His hair was that slick feathery black that glossed white
in the sun, his skin dark gold; he must have been a Caddo
Indian child from the reservation she'd passed a few miles
up the road. There was no one with him and she was road-
lonely and it seemed that God had put him there for her. A
foundling. And she was grateful. She opened her car door
and gestured and he padded barefoot towards her, innocent
and dumb as an infant. He was mute—when she asked his
name he pointed at his throat and shook his head. As they
drove she talked to him about everything that had happened
to her, ceaselessly, like a dam breaking open, sometimes
crying with the relief of it. The wind whipped her tears up
the sides of her face. She bought him ice cream and hot dogs
and let him lean as far out of the window as he wanted and
he laughed soundlessly, his mouth wide open. He pointed
emphatically to a river so she stopped and he dove in
without hesitation. In the water he melted and shape-shifted.
She sat on the hood of the car with her chin in her hand
and watched him for hours. After this she stopped at every
body of water they passed. She called him frog, water dog,
salamander, platypus. The word platypus made him laugh his
silent laugh so this is what she called him most often. Then
all at once he went motionless and would not eat or swim.
Even in the canned heat of the car she could feel a hectic
fever teeming from his skin, so she stopped at a motel.

In the infinite circular silence of the room time expands
and collapses like a lung. She begins to hear her mother's

voice from inside the walls, what you do to yourself is an abomination, it is an abomination unto the Lord, and unto yourself and the body God gave you, and she feels the blood rushing into her head hanging upside down off the bed the way she used to when her mother caught her with boys or drugs, until her eyes beat like hearts and her ears howled with blood. The sun slips its noose and night rises again and again, a wheel rolling endlessly over her, and she smokes and sleeps and dreams of death and cries over the body of platypus, her animal, her foundling, her abomination, until it comes clear as lightning that God is punishing her for caging him. The fever hovers over him palpably like a hand and she sees that it is his soul and that he is heartbroken, a water animal in dry captivity. She must release him, he must reclaim his lost heart. She smokes the last grain she has and rolls him into the cheap blanket. Headlights off, windows down so the night pours in and dilutes the cloistered white reek of infection coming from his body, she drives into the yawning dark. Mercy peace silence, she says in her small broken voice, it is an abomination, I will reverse this abomination of myself and of platypus with mercy peace silence. She scans the landscape for the black glint of water and in her mind she sees him already under the surface, fighting loose from the tangle of blanket to cut deeper towards the pulse of the earth, dead and whole and beautiful; and she, redeemed.

AN ABOMINATION OF PLATYPUS

by Cameron C. Pierce

In the House of Agonies, the amputee removes his pants. He crawls onto the bed to the woman, who is tied up and could not move if she tried. He sits on her face, grinding his corncob asshole into her nose.

The amputee never sprays or splatters. His shit is consistently firm. Sometimes the woman can tell what he has eaten. Today his shit tastes like pickled radish.

She chews the shit that has dropped into her mouth. She swallows delicately, with great care. If she does not swallow delicately and with great care, he will bring in the leopard or sometimes the platypus. The platypus can do terrible things to her. The platypus is much worse than the amputee or the leopard.

The amputee turns over and jams his cock between her lips and down her throat, gagging her. She throws up a little because the amputee enjoys that. He says it makes for a more labial dick-suck. She does not believe he knows the definition of the word labial.

"Ocean trembles like jelly in a jar," the amputee tells her. He often talks while doing things to her. She sucks and throws up a little bit more because, after all, he is practically choking her. "Schmucks out there on Corinthian Island with their rich hussy wives squirting tropical punch out of their pussies. Fuckin' shriveled sagging tits blackened by the sun. These rich white women have nigger tits. Meanwhile, their husbands are becoming saints of flaccidity. Nobody to titty-fuck 'em so they got to rub on each other with slimy fish they buy at the island market. Ever been titty-fucked by a fish?"

He slips his cock out of her mouth and jabs the purple head into her eyeless socket.

"That's how it feels. Like being poked in the eye."

He plunges his cock further into the socket. Her skull aches, veins of agony branching out from the bone around the missing eye.

The platypus is responsible for removing the eye. That was a long time ago.

In a month, the amputee will chew a hole through the woman's belly and fill the wound with milk and Wheaties, then eat. He will put her body on display in the storefront window of a baby clothing store in the abandoned Pearl District. He will hide a baby shoe inside her cunt. The woman knows none of this as the amputee ejaculates into her eyeless socket.

She knows it is probably impossible, but she swears she can feel semen on her brain.

As he pulls out, he tells her that she is special.

The room downstairs off the main entryway is full of skin and teeth. The floor is made of glass. Nobody enters this room except for the platypus, and only on Sundays.

Behind the platypus's back, the amputee and the leopard call this room The Church. The platypus knows of this, for the platypus knows everything that goes on in the House of Agonies, but the platypus does not let on that he knows.

This room full of skin and teeth is where the platypus checks on his investment portfolio.

There is a computer buried under the skin and teeth. The platypus clears away a little spot and presses his face against the glass floor. There, beneath the skin and teeth and the glass floor, the computer tells him how his investments are doing. Sometimes they do well. More often, they do poorly. The platypus has no power or control over his investments. Despite frequent diggings through the skin and teeth, he has not been able to find a keyboard or a mouse in the room. His claws won't break the glass, and an invisible wall over the doorway blocks anyone or anything but the platypus himself from entering the room. He tried to drag a chair in once and it burst into flames.

On the second floor, there is the amputee and the woman's room. Sometimes the amputee calls in the leopard or the platypus to do things to the woman. Mostly they keep to themselves.

The platypus occupies the sole room on the third floor. Like The Church, nobody except the platypus goes there.

The leopard lives in the coat closet. He dreams of eating the greedy platypus, who hordes two rooms while he, a cat of the jungle, must sleep among ski poles. The coat closet is full of ski poles, despite the suspicious absence of skis. Any time the leopard moves the ski poles out of the closet, they find their way back in again. The leopard hopes to utilize the ski poles in a plot to kill the platypus and move into The Church. The leopard has never set foot on the third floor, but he estimates it to be the ideal size for a library. Yes, the leopard will move into The Church and remodel the third floor into a library to house his book. It's true. The leopard is writing a book. It is called AN ABOMINATION OF PLATYPUS. If only he knew how to begin.

AN ABOMINATION OF PLATYPUS

by Mike Topp

I can
write a
poem
about
anything.

This
one is
about an
abomination
of
platypus.

TAXONOMY

PLATYPUS

Kingdom: Animalia
Phyylum: Chordata
Class: Mammalia
Order: Montremata
Family: Ornithorhynchidae
Genus: Ornithorhynchus
Species: O. anatinus

OTHER ANIMALS TO STUDY AND WHY

Okapi: Invisibility
Praying Mantis: Kills and eats mates
Black Widow Spider: Kills and eats mates
Wolves: Same as dogs
Thylacine: Extinct
Bengal Tiger: Biggest cat
Termites: Proctodeal prophylaxis
Sea Turtle: 20 mph (fastest reptile)
Ants: Social structure
Blue Whale: Largest mammal ever
Mosquito: Pest
Dragonfly: Predator and helicopter
Mites:
Butterflies and Moths: (Lepidoptera) Diapause and
metamorphosis

```
                                           ,=.
                        ,="""""==._____.="   o".____
            ,=.==''                              _____/
      ,==.,"                      ,  \,===""
  <        ,==)   \"'"=._.==)    \
    `=='' '      `"                  `"


                                        ,=.
                     ,="""""==._____.="   o".____
         ,=.==''                              _____/
   ,==.,"                      ,  \,===""
<        ,==)   \"'"=._.==)    \
  `=='' '      `"                  `"
```

FUCK YOU

✛

A platypus is at the police station. He's telling the officer on duty about how he was just drugged and robbed. "It was these two turtles!" the platypus sobs. "They beat me and took my money!" The officer asks, "Did you get a good look at them?" The platypus says, "No! It all happened so fast!"

✛

EXTRAS FOR EXPERTS

Slowly come to believe that the biggest problem in the world could have been solved when it was small, and build a shoebox diorama illustrating these principles. Check with your parents before impregnating anyone. You might like to replace the lid on the box with a pillow. Remember to use non-toxic paint, or don't. It really doesn't matter.

+

A STORY

An old man went for a walk in the park although he didn't know why. Then he crossed the street and yelled at a crazy old woman. The old woman fell down. Since then, the squirrels are gray in the summer.

+

In the privacy of his home Jesus wore slacks.

+

+INSECTS+
+AND+
+SO+
+FORTH+
++

+

A HIVE OF BEES

by DJ Berndt

You can't recall when the bees began swarming from your left pants pocket. You can't say for certain why this is happening or why you were chosen, but you have every reason to suspect the right pocket too.

+

Start by trying to clean the house. Pick up after yourself. You wash the dishes, you mow the grass, vacuum the carpet, but it still isn't yours.

They build in your bedroom closet. You hear their noises, still foreign to you, as you are in bed at night. Every once in a while, through the creaking and the buzzing and the song of their small and constant flight, you hear a name and see a shape. As your consciousness flees, you realize that maybe they are trying to tell you something, to teach you something even, but you can feel that you aren't yet ready to learn.

The paint above your bedpost is starting to peel as honey oozes from the walls. You scrape it off until eventually, in your own handwriting, you read: *no one will tell the difference anymore because there isn't any.*

Once in a while, you receive a phone call. No one is ever there when you try to answer. You dial the operator and she explains it all to you again. The same thing about the disconnected number, the same thing about the Queen.

Somehow you can tell that this is just the beginning. You try to gather what thoughts remain. You'll have to do some footwork, despite the hunger, despite yourself.

Despite even the bees.

Trash builds from the kitchen and spills into the rest of the house. You haven't remembered to take it out in months. You can't recall what it felt like to sleep, or even to eat, but that doesn't seem to matter anymore. Not with the weight of the wings. Not with the stinger and its hollow, poison shrillness.

Then finally, maddened by the pollen, you are able to forget your name.

Finish by trying to open your eyes. Try as hard as you can. Try to open your mind, open your heart, your hands, ears, mouth, anything. You can't. You are no longer just you. You belong to the hive now.

✦

Blind, mute, crawling through the tunnels you have built. Next to yourself, in front of yourself, beside yourself. You are all around now and you finally understand: *you are everyone and everyone is you.*

A PLAGUE OF LOCUSTS

by Frank Hinton

What was there to do but watch? I watch myself in the river. There is no shape to me, no color. The sun barely makes me out. The ripples can't still for even a moment. I'm hoping for some calm and an honest glimpse of what I look like. A brown lump wiggles in gold wet.

My mother smashed all of the mirrors in the house, she found even the jagged scrap I'd saved for myself. I came home one day and she made me watch her grind it beneath her boot. It became a thousand pieces smaller.

I just want to comb my hair. I want to smile at myself and think "pretty." This brown refraction does nothing. I scratch at the water with my nails. I feel heat on my fingers and draw back. I'm ugly. I stand and turn toward home.

There are bodies all over now, unburied and unnamed. Nick and I used to pick through their pockets and collect treasures. I still have a silver pocket knife, a roll of coins, a soapstone pipe. One day while listening to his flies, we picked through the pockets of a man not yet dead. He made a sound and rolled to us. His eyes were purple, black, gummy. He couldn't see us. When he opened his mouth things fell into deeper parts of his throat. We rolled back and he caught Nick's leg. I heard my brother scream and I turned and kicked the half-dead man and then Nick was released. The man stopped moving. We ran away and Nick kept choking out something. He said I'd killed the guy.

A bird falls from the sky. I watch the dust rise from the crash. The sky is gold now, but gold without shine. I walk toward my house imagining my reflection but my mind isn't working right. What do I look like? How old am I? What's my name? These things don't seem to matter now. Everything has wandered off.

In the house my mother chops at something, dinner. I watch her meaty fist around the knife. The house shakes off dust. I hope the old wood crumbles on us. She looks at me and looks away. I've nothing in my hands. Men on horses ride past and my mother drops the knife, metal on wood. She hurries to the window and looks out into the gold. I know who she wants to see, but my father isn't coming home.

Nick comes in an hour later and drops something onto the table.

"What's this?" mother asks. Nick says nothing.

She unwraps the package and sees red.

"Apples," she says as I mouth the same word. My mouth fills wet and I stumble forward and the three of us lean over the table to examine Nick's find.

"Down by Millbrook," Nick says. "A little tree you have to

climb around a cliff to find. Don't know how it lasted."

Locusts.

At night I lick my mouth for hours, licking at nothing like a dog. I think of those cans of apple juice you used to get. I think of pies with baked apples and caramel-covered apples and bobbing in a bucket for dozens of apples. Apples. Apples. I can see their reflection in the water.

In the middle of the night Nick kicks me awake.

"What? Are we in trouble?" I ask.

Nick pulls me up and takes me downstairs. The lantern burns and lights a figure: my fat mother on her back. Her tongue is laying outside of her mouth. Her dress is covered with continents of sweat. A trail of piss rolls from her legs. She's dead, I know, I've seen this pose a thousand times. I want to jump and cry.

We walk our way through the rest of the night. Nick and I carry all we own. Nothing can be seen in the morning. I can hear the creatures fucking all around me. At night the swarms get violent on one another. Swarming and fucking and swarming and fucking. We move in whatever direction we move. We move forward from whatever was taken away.

AN ECLIPSE OF MOTHS

by Carrie Seitzinger

One woman is late to board
with two tiny children,
and I give up my seat for them,
move to the back.
The steward slips me two
tiny bottles of vodka,
my own little glass family.

Let us all lean in one direction.

From inside this airplane,
as the cars grow toy-like,
so does the tragedy of your frown
or whatever I've done to
level the curl of your mouth.
What you look like from inside
the plane, nine miles away,
I can tell now, the ivory stones
that will someday become of your body,
how we live outside of ourselves,
how there is some end we're all nearing
and passing and nearing again,

some light that makes us feel like valleys.

Let us all face in one direction.

There is a wild moth, trapped on the flight,
flapping anxious, then settling
on the seat in front of me.
Those dust screens, pressed tightly together,
turn the whole creature to a speck.
Sometimes when our wings are the most open
is when we seem to disappear.

Let us all fly in one direction.

My small window like a missing tooth
gives way to a shrinking world,
and I can lonely imagine,
all the stinking hookers
you bought in my wake,
before you knew
this ship could come home,
before you ate my sweater,
unraveling it from one loose thread
like a whisper of moths, feasting.

How love is the animal
that does the destroying, the shaping,
but it is also the cloth
binding things together.

A CLOUD OF GRASSHOPPERS
+THE PLAGUE OF 1874+

by Christy Crutchfield

Inside, they can still hear the distinct sound of wings, a wooden sound, millions of tiny reeds slapping together at hummingbird speed. It's a sound that, though only her father has gone out in the cloud, sends the entire family to scratching.

A grasshopper is neither cricket nor cicada, but a grasshopper can be a locust. If it changes color. If it swarms.

The sisters were young enough, letting their bare legs fan out of their skirts on the porch. Then, a sudden grey cloud turned the sky hazy. Then, the sound of a storm. There was a strange smell of onion, and everything individualized. The cloud turned to thousands of advancing mouths, and the girls were rushed inside.

Their mother hands them a deck of cards. The occasional sound of a singular grasshopper breaks through the collective flitting and thumps against the window screen. They do not look at their father. A dress hem sliding along an ankle, an arm hair settling, it all makes the girls jump up from their game. They do not look out the window.

Most grasshoppers have wings for singing and not flying. The fabled grasshopper fiddles all summer and mocks the toiling ant. He starves to death in the winter.

+

When the reed sounds are finally gone, the light in the windows is brighter. Like a summer storm, there is still time for blue sky, white cloud. Her mother says the fire-crackling sound was not wings but jaws. They stay inside.

She listens for the cloud, many farms over. She didn't ask her father what it was like, trying to bat them away. She saw the tiny holes chewed into his shirt, kept quiet. There are red lines running down her sister's forearms.

In the morning, her mother picks at a dangling sleeve, the clothes on the line digested. The handles of rakes where the family left their sweat have been gnawed. They find the edges of their crop completely bare, but there are big patches in the middle where the corn was left fully intact. The neighbors' onion was completely destroyed. Another neighbor's potato untouched. More tornado than a cloud, she thinks.

There is also the fabled hen who was forced to bake bread all alone. She, like the ant, leaves the lazy unfed. It seems the moral of these stories is not hard work, but that hard work gives you the right to let others starve.

Her mother wraps her sister's hands in socks to keep her from scratching.

+

She grabs the rake. She will work through blisters to set this right. She will work until her thighs are strong and sore. She will marry the right man. Her father puts a rough hand on her head. What can a rake do, he says, it can't do anything. She thinks, the next time she sees a grasshopper, she will eat it. It's only fair.

When she hears him on the porch, she freezes. A single member, left behind. He is not green, but a copper color, dipped in bronze. His eyes and head twitch like some kind of machine. But when he bounds away and then, clicking, flies, she thinks what looked like machinery was actually muscle. She thinks he couldn't have been more than two inches long. She thinks, if she didn't stop to think about what he was, she could have crunched him under her boot.

She listens for the cloud, counties away by now, but only hears cicadas. She watches her socked sister sneak the dull side of the pencil to her neck. A year ago, this happened. You couldn't walk a foot without a huge cicada thudding against your head. Husks on every tree. But these bugs were less interested in crops, and more in sex and then dying. And this cloud was a cloud of Rocky Mountain Locusts. She imagines pencil splinters settling into her sister's neck.

In Mexico, men lure grasshoppers with bright lamps and gather them in nets. They fry and eat them with chili and lime.

+

Her sister's legs are pale on the porch, already showing blotches of pink. But she keeps her own covered, her parents squeezing her shoulders, calling it maturity. Her mother calls

a woman who hops from man to man *a grasshopper.* Those
women, in their own winters, meet the fate of the fable. Her
daughter is becoming a woman and must be listening.

Decades later, when America believes itself immune, it will
fight these clouds with poison.

Throughout the summer, they find occasional strays, copper
mementos of the plague. Her father saves one under glass, a
bronzed trophy. It's just the length of her palm with armored
thigh muscle, a complicated mouth hung open. It's pinned
right through where the heart would be, if grasshoppers were
anything like humans.

More decades later, perhaps due to new plowing techniques,
the Rocky Mountain Locust will be extinct.

What her mother will never know is that even into
September, she will hide a sticky sore on her upper thigh.
Beneath her skirt. Raw from scratching.

AN ARMY OF CATERPILLARS

by Matt Hill

Lindsay is here to eat the Eiffel Tower.

Paris is peeled, cored, rotting. Lindsay walks across its brazed
face like a clockwork penguin. He wears a protective suit
on account of the bad weather. In these parts, you can still
measure the wind with a Geiger counter.

Lindsay struggles. The lead lining creaks behind the knees.
He doesn't see anybody, won't expect to.

The suit's recyclers hiss and suck. He looks up—it doesn't go
dark anymore, just a different shade of yellow.

Only Lindsay knows why he wants to eat the Eiffel Tower.
Probably it's on the whim of some vision, maybe a mineral
deficiency, but the gap between wanting and doing is getting
thin. It's simply that the idea is unshakeable. It's a fixation.

So he scrambles through toppled worlds and turned-out
roads. Signs blasted off shops, wires torn out, coiled into
nooses. Felled pillars and fused cars. Between alleys and the
holes in walls, glances of the tower. He weeps. His suit won't

go faster—

And there, in the open. The tower like some rocket's skeleton on a used launchpad. The park beneath scorched black, glassy.

Closer, squatting in a crater, he flicks through photos for reference. It's true: the park was wiped clean off. The tower hasn't done so badly, but it's bent at the tip. It's become a grim sort of net, with chunks of buildings caught in the mesh.

Lindsay strips. The gloves, the boots. The zip running from neck to calves. He's in an under-suit; rags mainly. He begins to run.

The bomb-gilded tower throws long shadows, spearing for a moon you can't see for cloud. Lindsay scuffs his way up a stone foot. Up close, paint curls from the structure.

He pauses. He puts a hand against his meal. It hums, all four legs against the shearing wind. He looks into the iron lattice, its belly, the kaleidoscope frame. It sings up his arm—songs spanning 1889 to now. His knees weak before this black sentinel, and all these dreams dreamt under it.

He bites. Tentative at first, a taster. The paint on his tongue. He relaxes; his jaw clicks. The tears on his cheeks. Again, harder. The pressure through his gums, cheeks. Harder, that first crack. The first split. Till his teeth come free. He chews, gnaws; runs his gums up and down the leg. His chin black and shiny. He tastes the copper; the iron and the tears.

+

After, he rests in his crater. Back in his suit, exposure forgotten. The tower groans while he takes drugs for the pain. He induces sleep.

+

On waking, a dog with a man attached to it. The man is faceless, also suited. He clears his visor.

Lindsay nearly shoots him.
The man swears in French. He looks sad. He says, Why are you here?

Lindsay laughs. The crust on his chin cracks and flakes away. He dips inside his suit, pulls out a leaf. It's vacuum-bagged, still green. He points out the holes in it, the polka-dot pattern spreading through its fibres. He holds it up against the tower, smiling. He traces the lattice-work of the leaf, its structure. The browned edges of the circles bitten into it.

And he tells the man why he's here.

The man looks between the leaf and the tower. He says, I'm with people. We saw—
Lindsay pockets the leaf. Good, he says. Then let me tell you again.

+

A dozen people scale the tower's feet. Soon, their teeth carpet the stone.

Together they chew and bleed and wait. An army of caterpillars, desperate to become.

A PAIL OF WASPS

by Brian Carr

the paper wasps had homed the pail. the punishment was simple. they weren't to be killed. their hive would come alive when i touched the handle. their wings would shimmy with anger, their colony about to flurry with war. i'd wrecked gram's car. drinking. the pail would be moved across the yard. if gingerly done, would they not sting? gram had perched a lawn chair to see. my body slicked with sweat. "couldn't i just pay the damages? i've got money enough," she said, "this kinda entertainment you don't stumble on casually." "what if i'm allergic? i ain't never been stung to know." "what if," she said and lit a marlboro. my heart beat frantic. their gray-paper colony, a weird house of poison forthcoming. they spit up into the air in wild patterns as i lifted. gram gave a chuckle, her aged humor aching my ears. i peered at her. she must have sensed it. "don't you dare," she said, her words stained with tobacco smoke, her face streaked fearful. i lobbed, and the pail slammed her lap. she fell into a gray mess of oldness screaming, her pale cotton clothes in heaps about her. "you're right," i said to gram. "this is awfully entertaining." i walked away casual and since haven't been back.

A LOVELINESS OF LADYBUGS

by Mel Bosworth

In the morning they apply
their moisturizer.
They think about you first,
how you will dress
them with your eyes.

Will you make them
wear raincoats again
or bonnets? Will you
strip them entirely
in order to count their spots?
It's a myth, you know,
that the spots mark age
like tree rings.

Headlights, dim
as the engines
behind them.
They are not
cars. This is how
they move now.

Above you, the ceiling
slides to the left, hundreds
of black legs scuttling.
They carry their beauty slowly,
a beach bound Volkswagen
sun split and sandy.

Pretty faces. Sticky palms.
Genies with domed red backs.
Make a wish. We're all dying.
You have candy, fuck-o.

A GRIST OF BEES

by Poncho Peligroso

After the snow melted that year, there was an unprecedented surge in the number of ghost bees as they began to hatch from their little ghost bee eggs in springtime abundance. Had the ghost bees been corporeal, they would have seemed to block out the sun, so great was their number. Their overpopulation was such that a claustrophobic panic arose among them despite their being acclimated to the incredible density of beehives already. As a result, the ghost bees became unusually aggressive, much like the "killer" African ghost bees, and began to attack ghost humans.

Had any living eyes been capable of seeing this phenomenon, they would behold nightmarish clouds of ghost bees stinging ghost humans to double-death. This resulted in the attacking ghost bees double-dying as well from the trauma of stinging, causing a vicious cycle of bees and humans attacking each other into futile perpetuity across innumerable levels of death, each with exponentially increased ghostiness. This ectoplasmic war was set to the dulcet tones of the deafening buzz of untold ghost bees and the agonized screams of pain from slightly-more-told-but-still-largely-untold ghost humans. However, as no living person was capable of perceiving these ghosts, the surge of fresh ghost bee eggs that spring was noted by the general public as a decline in the amount of living bees for reasons as of then undetermined by science.

The terror and unease elicited by ghost humans attempting to interact directly with living humans was inconspicuously absent, but the ghost bees, despite operating on ghost bee instinct that was similar to vengeance but not complex enough (lacking human motivations and seething resentments and such) to evoke any unease in humans, still managed to reach us. Though they did not register on an emotional or physical level, the ghost bees did, however, register in our world as an inexplicably password-free broadband internet connection across the whole of the North American continent, which various wireless telecommunications companies scrambled to somehow take credit for. All this was an unintended side effect of one (living) man's love, devotion, and fear of modern transportation technology taken to the extreme.

This man, the cause of the decline of the living bee population, was oblivious to his work receiving any attention from the scientific community or general public. His intended audience was one woman and he did not follow the news, having been far too busy. He had only wanted to see his love again, which would have been a simple endeavor were he not intensely phobic of most modern mass-transit options and without a car. The last time he had seen her, before she was taken away by time and circumstance, they laid on the grass together, he on his back, her head on his chest. The snow had melted and it was the first clear day of spring, but she hid her eyes from the light as she cried into his chest. He wanted to hold her close to his chest just as she was and to look into her eyes simultaneously, which would require an implausible level of neck flexibility from him. Instead, he held her close and stared straight up where the sky above was the same piercing deep blue as her eyes. For a moment, his mind stayed silent and comforted, unable to think of the departure and distance between him and his love, as the enveloping sky seemed so like the color of her eyes as she smiled with love that he could not conceive of being without her on any clear day. He held this peace until a bee landed on the inside of his glasses, eliciting a panic that brought concerns of mortality and loneliness back to the forefront of his mind. He shook off the bee and she comforted him and he comforted her until she had to go. They stood and walked.

She said she would wait and so he set out to walk across the continent towards her, being able to sense where she was in the same way that birds can instinctively guide themselves by the Earth's magnetic field. He tried his thumb at hitchhiking, but found his luck was terrible, as he was uniformly ejected from highways and on-ramps by law enforcement before he could get any helpful rides. Forced to walk, he walked. As he did, he encountered living, corporeal bees occasionally bothering him along his path, besmirching his view of his love's eyes in the sky. His fight-or-flight instinct came in, but as his goal and mode of transit was so clear and decisive, he would not allow himself the option of flight, and therefore fought the bees, punching them from the air one at a time.

Never one to halfass a project, he continued toward his love via circuitous route designed to optimize the destruction of bees. Through rain and shine, he forged forward, fists flying into living bees, facing down entire hives in whirlwinds of pinpoint-precise punches. Almost inaudible "thwaps" accompanied the death of each bee he struck down, and, for a long time, he was never stung, as his kung-fu was strong. In his wake he left a conspicuous absence of buzzing or pollination, which slowly grew to the attention of the rest of the world. He wanted to bring her the freshest flowers and make her home an Eden, and to do that he would have to ensure that there were no other fresh flowers but hers, and without the bees he would be sure of this. He fought on and the ectoplasmic bleed of the Wi-Fi signal grew stronger, though its signal alerted and angered the remaining bees, who all knew that he was coming for them. They prepared. After a long time he grew close to his goal, his love, only to find an insurmountable wall of bees coming for him, emitting the deafening buzz and darkening the sky like their ghost-bee brethren had done without any living witnesses. The bees could sense him coming and he could sense his love somewhere beyond them. He faced toward them and walked forward, hoping for a Red Sea scenario brought about by the power of love, but was engulfed in the bees, filled with poison and lifted up towards the pure blue of the sky in the last moments of his life. He reached up and stretched his arm and continued out through his own fingertip into a cloud of bees bigger than the one he had emerged from, all invisible and vivid at once, ghost bees swarming and carrying him once again. His ghost fell into the Wi-Fi signal like the bees he'd brought into it before him, and the signal stretched to find her. As the signal, he was everywhere at once, but tried to transmit himself to her alone, constantly pouring through her at the speed of light and carrying information about his love, but silent and invisible, inaccessible and unusable by the human body. She could not wait forever, he knew, but she would never want for high-speed internet again, and in the meantime he fell through layers of death until he managed to placate the bees, and now sits somewhere beyond the veil, waiting for his love to join him, and tending a hive to ensure the health of the season's new ghost bee eggs.

A CRACKLE OF CRICKETS

by Gabriel Blackwell

As David Box awoke one 1960 morning from uneasy dreams, he found himself transformed into a gigantic insect.

3 yrs prior, Buddy Holly, disappointed by the inception & reception of 2 eponymous Decca sides, rerecorded them with producer Norman Petty.

Contractually, Holly couldn't release the new versions under his own name, so he & his bandmates turned to the encyclopedia for a new one.

Holly, big fan of The Orioles, tried to find a suitable and unused bird name, but that didn't fly with his bandmates, stuck on The Spiders.

The group compromised: an insect, but one that flew—The Crickets. The Beetles was tried but scrapped (they get squashed, JI Allison said).

They had evidently not read the encyclopedia entry for Gryllidae very closely. No matter—they were flying high.

2 albums, both smash hits, were released in less than 3 months: "The Chirping Crickets" (by The Crickets) & "Buddy Holly" (by Buddy Holly).

Chirping can serve several purposes, but is primarily used by the male cricket as a way of calling the female and warning off other males.

Holly departed for NYC alone, reconstituting himself as "Buddy Holly"; Crickets Allison and Mauldin couldn't see leaving Lubbock.

Crickets' wings are useless as motor or even rudder; they are instead instrument and amplifier of the sound commonly known as "chirping."

Touring under his own name, Holly boarded an overnight flight to Moorhead, Minnesota on 2/2/59. The plane crashed. There were no survivors.

As tribute to his fallen idol, Box recorded a few Crickets songs under the name The Ravens and sent the resulting demos to Allison.

Chirps heard in concert are usually warnings to other males, oneupsmanship. They get inexorably more strident as more crickets join in.

Allison invited Box to join he and Mauldin at their next recording session. Result? Crickets 45: Don't Cha Know b/w Peggy Sue Got Married.

Box was admitted to the School of American Art, his application perhaps involving the portraiture of an anthropomorphized creature. Cricket?

The school was located in Westport, CT, 50 miles—a short hop—from the NYC apt. where Holly's wife, Maria Elena, became a widow in '59.

Maria Elena heard of the crash thru the squawks of an ill-tuned radio, before anyone thought to phone her. She miscarried Holly's child.

Chirps heard in isolation are the result of lonely desperation, the closest the insect world comes to balladeering.

Box returned to Texas & to music in '64, performing under his own name and touring with a drummer certified to pilot small aircraft.

Box's flight home to Lubbock after his last gig in Houston crashed on 10/23/64, killing everyone onboard.

A cricket can be heard after the final refrain of Holly's I'm Going to Love You Too, the one that begins, You're going to say you miss me.

Coming at the very end of the fade-out, the chirp is virtually indistinguishable from the cymbal-crash that precedes it.

The Crickets were unaware of its presence until the track was mixed. Petty wanted to remove it, but the group wouldn't allow him.

They were still laboring under the misapprehension that crickets produce chirps with their legs, that their wings were for flying.

A COLONY OF TERMITES

by Michael Kimball

We knew that the old Victorian house needed work when we bought it. The wood floors needed to be stripped and refinished. The rotting planks on the wrap porches needed to be replaced so that we didn't fall through them. We had to be careful about where we stepped then. We were just putting our marriage back together again after what we called the difficult years.

It was the beginning of a muggy summer when we moved into our new house and we slept with the windows open. We could hear the richness of insects listing at the window screens. We listened to the police helicopters whirring up over the city and sometimes their spotlights would shine through the windows of the house. After the city quieted, we could hear a chattering of rats out in the back garden—chirps, squeaks, and tiny screams. My wife read in the local newspaper about a whole network of rat tunnels running under the city. We lived on top of that.

We were house poor, but after the summer got hotter we bought a window unit for the master bedroom so that we could sleep at night. We were only living in certain rooms then and we didn't mind the heat in the rest of the house, which didn't feel like it was ours yet anyway.

After we rebuilt the wrap porches, we tried to eat dinner outside under the porch light, but there seemed to be an infusion of insects into the nighttime. There was a gathering of moths around the porch light and an orchestra of crickets that we could not see. We could hear the collection of June bugs feeding in the garden and we kept slapping at the air around us to knock down the squadron of mosquitoes that wanted to feed on us.

After we became accustomed to the low hum of the window unit in our bedroom, we noticed that our old Victorian house made all kinds of night noises. At first, we assumed that it was the house settling around us, but it wasn't too long after that when we realized how active the walls of the house were at night. We thought it was probably a scamper of mice or maybe a carriage of baby possums. We weren't even sure that we were hearing those insistent intonations or if they were something inside us.

One morning, we started peeling off the layers of wallpaper that covered the plaster walls. The intricate patterns of the wallpaper were from different decades than the one we were living in and we were trying to get down to the bones of the house. The wall plaster fell down in dusty chunks as we peeled the wallpaper and revealed the slatted wood walls. It was there that we found the first evidence of a colony of termites, the wood slats grooved with tunnels and chambers. We didn't see any actual termites, just small hills of sawdust and little piles of dried termite wings. Apparently, the colony of termites had found our house years before us and entered through the unsealed foundation. We were an intrusion of humans.

A BUSINESS OF FLIES

by xTx

Meat, lots of meat. In the sun. Dead things. A dead cat's eye.
A dead deer's eye. A dead dog's eye. A dead rat's exploded
guts. A sandy fish. A rotting pigeon. A baby bird sticking
with twigs. A body broken and bloody. A body broken by
a collapse. A body broken by a train. A body broken by a
fall. A body broken. A body. A pie, sitting out. A cheese
tray. A plate of nachos. My sandwich. My potato salad. My
barbecued chicken leg. A pile of shit, un-stepped on. A pile
of shit, stepped on. A pile of shit. A place above the trash
pile. A place beside the trash pile. A place behind the trash
pile. The trash pile. Trash. A black boy's starving face. A
brown boy's starving face. An ivory girl's starving face. A
starving face. A face. An eye. A nose. A mouth. A tongue. An
untended wound. A horse. A cow. A lamb. A goat. Summer
day skin. Walls. Countertops. Armchairs. Jelly globs. The
snot-string across my grandfather's cheek. The ice cream
cone dropped by a blind girl. A collapsed lung in the person
you love the most. The place where mothers leave. The way
you can't go back again. The day you finally accept none
of your wishes will ever come true. How you'll never, ever
measure up. The disappointment in his eyes. The forever of
these things and how

you can

never

completely

wave them off.

ABOUT THE AUTHORS

Andrew Borgstrom, Ashley-Elizabeth Best, Ben Tanzer, Bradley Sands, Brian Carr, Caitlin Laura Galway, Cameron C. Pierce, Carrie Seitzinger, Chelsea Laine Wells, Christy Crutchfield, Colleen Elizabeth Rowley, Crispin Best, David Doc Luben, David Drury, David Tomaloff, DJ Berndt, Frances E. Dinger, Frank Hinton, Gabriel Blackwell, Hazel Cummings, J. A. Tyler, J. Bradley, Jamie Iredell, Janey Smith, Jarrid Deaton, Jess Dutschmann, Jess Rowan, Jessica Knauss, Jim Ruland, Joseph Riippi, Kevin Sampsell, Kirsten Alene Pierce, Lauren Tamraz, Len Kuntz, Lindsay Allison Ruoff, Matt Ferner, Matt Hill, Matthew Simmons, Matty Byloos, Maurice Burford, Megan Lent, Mel Bosworth, Michael Kimball, Mike Topp, Morris Hawthorne, Nate Quiroga, Nicky Tiso, Peter Schwartz, Poncho Peligroso, Riley Michael Parker, Robert Duncan Gray, Robert Vaughan, Robyn Bateman, Ryan Boyd, Ryan W. Bradley, Stephen Tully Dierks, Suzanne Burns, Ted Powers, Tom De Beauchamp, Tyler Gobble, Willie Fitzgerald, xTx, and yt sumner are writers living in America or Canada or Australia or what have you with a wife or a boyfriend or two kids or a cat or a cactus or some combination of those things. He or she either has a job or goes to some sort of school or kind of just floats through life somehow, possibly on a trust fund, possibly on unemployment. Most of these people like movies and/or music. Some of them have living parents. Some of them own their own car. More or less, everyone is the same, yeah? Yeah. If you want to know more about the writers featured in this book, or anyone else for that matter, might we suggest the internet?

RECOMMENDED READING

MEAT IS ALL by Andrew Borgstrom
YOU CAN MAKE HIM LIKE YOU by Ben Tanzer
RICO SLADE WILL FUCKING KILL YOU by Bradley Sands
LOST IN CAT BRAIN LAND by Cameron C. Pierce
I DON'T RESPECT FEMALE EXPRESSION by Frank Hinton
A MAN OF GLASS & ALL THE WAYS WE HAVE FAILED by J. A. Tyler
PROSE. POEMS. A NOVEL by Jamie Iredell
DODGING TRAFFIC by J. Bradley
BIG LONESOME by Jim Ruland
THE ORANGE SUITCASE by Joseph Riippi
A COMMON PORNOGRAPHY by Kevin Sampsell
LOVE IN THE TIME OF DINOSAURS by Kirsten Alene Pierce
THE MOON TONIGHT FEELS MY REVENGE by Matthew Simmons
DON'T SMELL THE FLOSS by Matty Byloos
FREIGHT by Mel Bosworth
US by Michael Kimball
SHORTS ARE WRONG by Mike Topp
THE ROMANTIC by Poncho Peligroso
OUR BELOVED 26TH by Riley Michael Parker
PRIZE WINNERS by Ryan W. Bradley
MISFITS AND OTHER HEROES by Suzanne Burns
NORMALLY SPECIAL by xTx

RECOMMENDED WEBSITES

HOUSEFIRE	www.housefirepublishing.com
METAZEN	www.metazen.ca
PANK	www.pankmagazine.com
SMALLDOGGIES	www.smalldoggiesmagazine.com
HTML GIANT	http://htmlgiant.com
POP SERIAL	www.popserial.tumblr.com
UNICORN KNIFE FIGHT	www.unicornknifefight.com
MUD LUSCIOUS	www.mudlusciouspress.com
FUTURE TENSE	www.futuretensebooks.com
LAZY FASCIST	http://lazyfascist.com/
DOGZPLOT	http://dogzplot.blogspot.com
PANGUR BAN PARTY	www.pangurbanparty.com

MISSING NOUNS OF ASSEMBLAGE
+WE COULDN'T FIND ANYONE TO WRITE THESE+

A CORNUCOPIA OF SLUGS

A CLUTTER OF CATS

A RAFTER OF TURKEY

A YOKE OF OX

A BAND OF COYOTE

A PACK OF RATS

A GULP OF MAGPIE

A DRIFT OF HOG

A BED OF OYSTER

A PACE OF ASS

+WE+
+WILL+
+DESTROY+
+YOU+
++